LANGUAGE ARTS 1007
MEDIEVAL ENGLISH I

MW01122552

CONTENTS

Author: **Helen Robertson Prewitt, MA.Ed.**
Editor: Alan Christopherson, M.S.
Illustrator: Alpha Omega Graphics

Alpha Omega Publications®

804 N. 2nd Ave. E., Rock Rapids, IA 51246-1759

ENGLISH 1205
MEDIEVAL ENGLISH LITERATURE

One of the reasons Americans study about England is that American literature and history have their roots in England. Through tracing America's cultural heritage, you can come to a better understanding of what America is and what America hopes to become. Many of the standards, ideas, and concepts Americans hold dear are derived from much earlier times. Early settlers brought with them the English tradition, which is actually a blending of ideas from many different societies.

This LIFEPAC® will present the historical changes and developments as well as the literary achievements for three major periods in England. First, you will study the early period in which the Old English language developed. You will discover the relationships between history, language changes, and literary development during this time.

Next, you will become aware of the impact the Norman invasion had upon Anglo-Saxon society in its government, its language, its population, and its literature. This second section will deal with changes occurring between the years A.D. 1066 and A.D. 1300.

Finally, you will deal with fourteenth-century England and its greatest literary representative, Geoffrey Chaucer. You will study the many influences upon the literature of this period. Chaucer's literature is great because it portrays a cross section of medieval society, making these people understandable and interesting. You may be surprised to learn that some of these fourteenth-century characters resemble some twentieth-century people.

OBJECTIVES

Read these objectives. The objectives tell you what you will be able to do when you have successfully completed this LIFEPAC.

When you have completed this LIFEPAC, you should be able to:

1. Explain the contributions to language and literature made by the early Britons, the Celts, the Romans, and the Anglo-Saxons.

2. Identify characteristics of the Old English language.

3. Explain the role of the poet and the oral tradition in Anglo-Saxon society.

4. Identify and describe the Anglo-Saxon literary forms of epic, elegy, riddle, and gnomic verse.

5. Recognize pagan and Christian elements in Anglo-Saxon literature.

6. Explain the impact of the Norman conquest upon Anglo-Saxon society, language, and literature.

7. Identify the importance of feudalism and the church as reflected by Chaucer's *Canterbury Tales*.

8. Describe the types of literature that dominated the transitional period between A.D. 1066 and A.D. 1300.

9. Recognize the Middle English language.

10. Identify Chaucer's writing and to summarize parts of the *Canterbury Tales*.

11. Identify other literary works of the fourteenth century.

Survey the LIFEPAC. Ask yourself some questions about this study. Write your questions here.

_____
_____
_____
_____
_____
_____
_____
_____
_____

I. EARLY ENGLAND

The early period of English history is revealed to us primarily through the literature and through certain archaeological discoveries. Before written history, stories about early people—their beliefs, their heroes, and their accomplishments—were preserved through the oral tradition.

In this section you will learn more about the early Britons who settled in the British Isles and the later invaders who brought with them new elements of language, new ideas, new beliefs, and new traditions. You will learn a little about each of the major invading tribes or groups. You will see how the Celts, the Romans, the Anglo-Saxons, and the Jutes influenced the Anglo-Saxon literature. You will learn more about the Old English language; the poet and the oral tradition; the epic and *Beowulf*; the elegy, represented by the "Wanderer" and the "Seafarer;" the riddle; and gnomic verse.

SECTION OBJECTIVES

Review these objectives. When you have completed this section, you should be able to:

1. Explain the contributions to language and literature made by the early Britons, the Celts, the Romans, and the Anglo-Saxons.
2. Identify characteristics of the Old English language.
3. Explain the role of the poet and the oral tradition in Anglo-Saxon society.
4. Identify and describe the Anglo-Saxon literary forms of epic, elegy, riddle, and verse.
5. Recognize pagan and Christian elements in Anglo-Saxon literature.

VOCABULARY

Study these words to enhance your learning success in this section.

alliterative	caesura
comitatus	kenning

Note: All vocabulary words in this LIFEPAC appear in **boldface** print the first time they are used. If you are unsure of the meaning when you are reading, study the definitions given.

EARLY HISTORY OF ENGLAND

The history of England should be fascinating to most Americans because many of the roots of our country are in England. A common misconception is that England has always been populated by people very much like today's Englishman. Nothing could be further from the truth. Many different people, from the Picts to the Normans, have inhabited the British Isles. The history of England is colorful and often violent. Each major influence or change in her culture and her population has been brought about by an invasion.

Early Britons. Little is known about the earliest inhabitants of the British Isles. This time period is mysterious because no written documents have been found detailing the lives and beliefs of the people. Later discoveries have uncovered certain artifacts, drawings, and manuscripts that have helped historians piece together more information about these early peoples. What is known is that the early Britons mined tin and made bronze tools and weapons. They may have built Stonehenge, a circular arrangement of huge stones. Stonehenge, located in Wiltshire, England, may have served as an observatory and as an astronomical calendar, accurately indicating the seasons and eclipses. Scientists and historians are still puzzled about the manner of construction of such an accurate and complicated calendar by a so-called barbarian people.

Stonehenge

The Celts. By 700 B.C. England was invaded by a group known as the Celts. Two groups of Celts developed in the British Isles. The first group was composed of the Irish, Scots, and Manx peoples who spoke a language variation known as Gaelic. The second group made up the Welsh, Carnish, and Britons who spoke Brythonic. These Celtic people were aggressive warriors who worshiped gods of nature. Their religion involved magic and perhaps even human sacrifice. The Celts made and dyed woolen cloth. They set up trade with other areas of Europe. When the Romans invaded England in 52 B.C., the Celts were forced into the hill country of northwestern England, thus escaping Latin influence. The Romans called one group of the Celts *Picts*, because they painted themselves blue. The word *pict* comes from the Latin word *pictus* meaning painted.

The Romans. The Roman Empire spread over most of the known world from northern Africa to most of Europe, from the Middle East to Spain, and even to Britain in the west. The Romans built their empire as a result of many wars. To hold their newly acquired possessions, Rome established outposts and built roads.

After his conquest of Gaul (present-day France), Julius Caesar directed his attentions toward Britain. Perhaps he had heard about the rich tin mines, woolen cloth, and other British resources from traders. Caesar was aware of the aid and protection the Britons had provided to his enemies, the Gauls. Caesar invaded Britain in 52 B.C. The Britons resisted, but they were conquered. England was occupied by Roman troops for about four hundred years. Britain still contains the remains of many Roman structures such as Hadrian's Wall, which was built by Romans in A.D. 120. They also built forts for protection against the inhabitants of Scotland.

England flourished under Roman rule. Roman-built roads encouraged trade and the growth of towns. London became an important port.

Complete these statements.

1.1 A circular monument devised by the early Britons is called _____ .

1.2 One tribe of Britons who painted themselves blue were called _____ .

1.3 Early British natural resources included a. _____ and b. _____ .

1.4 Julius Caesar invaded Britain in _____ B.C.

The Anglo-Saxons. When the Romans withdrew their troops from Britain to repel invaders attacking Rome, Britain was left unprotected. Other invaders threatened British inhabitants. Picts and Scots invaded from the North Sea. The Angles, Saxons, and Jutes invaded and settled in the southeastern part of Britain. The name Angle-Land, later England, was taken from the tribe called the Angles.

The Anglo-Saxon period extends from about A.D. 449 to A.D. 1066. The legendary King Arthur was supposed to have reigned about A.D. 500. The legend may have been based on the life of a real Celtic leader—a leader who organized the Britons against the Germanic invaders.

The Angles, Saxons, and Jutes were Germanic tribes that crossed the North Sea to conquer Britain. By the end of the sixth century, they had conquered the territory. These tribes settled in tiny regions. They had blended into larger kingdoms by A.D. 597 when Pope Gregory sent missionaries to England. An English nationalism came early to these kingdoms. Conversion to Christianity and a common bond to ward off invaders encouraged a national spirit.

The Anglo-Saxons, as these blended Germanic tribes came to be called, were hardy people. They were ruled by the traditional Germanic system of the leader, or chieftain, and his *witan*, or council of retainers. They called assemblies to discuss issues and to interpret laws.

The Anglo-Saxons were also an artistic people. Recent archaeological findings reveal that their craftsmen produced artifacts and ornaments such as brooches, helmets, and bracelets.

The year A.D. 597 marks the beginnings of English history. The English had learned from Roman and Irish missionaries to make written records of historical events. By then the language was actually called English, although scholars have used the term Anglo-Saxon to identify the language spoken at this time. Anglo-Saxon is closely related to Saxon and Frisian (Low German). Latin has influenced English through the church and through the classical writings. Danish (Scandinavian) influenced the language, especially in the tenth and eleventh centuries.

The spread of Christianity brought increased learning. Some men learned to read and write Latin while training for holy orders. Others studied Greek, the language used by the early church. Latin gradually replaced Greek in the West. By A.D. 597 a great deal of Christian literature as well as pagan and secular literature had been written in or translated into Latin. Monastic schools were established. Theodore, Archbishop of Canterbury, and the African Abbot Hadrian set up such a monastic school at Canterbury. Within a short time England became a leader in learning.

During this period of learning, a record of early history and culture was set down. The past was kept alive by reading and by recording events in books. This process was painstaking since the average scribe could copy only two books a year.

Some monks began to write their own books in Latin. Aldhelm (or Ealdhelm) who lived near the end of the seventh century was a monk from Wessex and a student of Theodore and Hadrian. Aldhelm, a poet, was the first English writer of importance. A few of his verses and poetic riddles remain today.

Benedict Biscop (A.D. 628–A.D. 690), a monk from Northumbria, worked with Theodore at Canterbury for a time. Then he returned to Northumbria to establish Benedictine monasteries. Venerable Bede, a student of Biscop, became the outstanding Anglo-Latin writer of the period. Bede entered the monastery when he was seven years old and remained there for the rest of his life. He wrote many types of works including accounts of the lives of saints, commentaries on the books of the Bible, scientific treatises, grammatical handbooks, and critical writings. His *Historia Ecclesiastica Gentis Anglorum, The Ecclesiastical History of the English Nation* is important for the information it provides about the transition of England from a barbarian to a civilized culture. Bede was a great historian and an outstanding scholar, yet he recorded many events that most histories might not contain. He was careful to investigate his material for accuracy. Methods of investigation at his time, however, were not developed; and standards of belief were different from those of the modern world. Therefore, some of his writings are considered legend. Nevertheless, Bede is considered the father of English history.

Egbert, a student of Bede, became Archbishop of York. He set up a great cathedral school that produced outstanding writers. One of these writers was Alcuin (A.D. 735–A.D. 804). Alcuin was brought to France by Charlemagne to help encourage the revival of learning during the Carolingian Renaissance.

Match these items.

1.5	_____ Anglo-Saxon period	a. father of English history
1.6	_____ missionaries sent by Pope Gregory	b. council of retainers
1.7	_____ Benedict Biscop	c. A.D. 597
1.8	_____ Venerable Bede	d. chosen by Charlemagne
1.9	_____ Alcuin	e. Celtic leader
1.10	_____ witan	f. A.D. 449-A.D. 1066
		g. teacher of Bede

The West Saxons, as the inhabitants of Wessex were called, had been fighting off Danish Viking invasions from about A.D. 787 to about A.D. 1017. These Viking attacks resulted in the establishment of Danish settlements in England. England seemed literally to be losing ground.

In A.D. 871 Alfred the Great became king of Wessex. He was an outstanding leader who brought peace to his country, saving it from conquest by the Danes. After several battles, Alfred defeated the Danes. Guthram, the Danish leader, was baptized as a Christian. Finally, Alfred established the Danelaw, which gave a portion of Eastern England to the Danes, but which restricted the Danes to that portion and no other.

Many monasteries and churches had been looted by the Danes. Because of this looting, education declined. Alfred drew on the monasteries for teachers and brought teachers in from other countries when necessary. He became a patron of educators and of students. Alfred also influenced education by translating books from Latin into Anglo-Saxon, the language of the people. Alfred began the *Anglo-Saxon Chronicle* in A.D. 892. This chronicle was the first account of history recorded in English (Old English) and is the oldest extant national chronicle. Alfred protected England by establishing forts, by being active in foreign affairs, and by keeping peaceful relations with his neighbors. He improved government by formulating a good code of laws.

Statue of Alfred the Great

Alfred's followers finally regained the Danelaw in A.D. 954. They ruled a united England until A.D. 1016 when King Canute captured England and made it part of the Danish kingdom. The English under Edward the Confessor again ruled England from A.D. 1042 to A.D. 1066 when the Norman Conquest dealt the death blow to much of Anglo-Saxon culture, language, and art. Gradually the language and customs of the Normans merged with the English, and the Middle English period was born.

Answer *true* **or** *false*.

1.11 _____ Danish Vikings invaded England from about A.D. 787 to about A.D. 1017.

1.12 _____ The Danelaw gave the Danes all of England.

1.13 _____ King Canute was an Anglo-Saxon king.

1.14 _____ Alfred began the *Anglo-Saxon Chronicle* in A.D. 892.

1.15 _____ The inhabitants of Wessex were called West Saxons.

Complete this activity.

1.16 Choose a topic from those listed. Search out more information about it. Either present your information as an oral report or turn in a paper that summarizes your findings.

| the Celts | King Arthur | King Alfred the Great | the Vikings |
| Stonehenge | Danelaw | Venerable Bede | |

Adult Check _____
            Initial   Date

6

EARLY LITERATURE OF ENGLAND

Few examples of Anglo-Saxon literature have survived. The Danes destroyed many manuscripts in their raids and destroyed entire monastic libraries. Surviving manuscripts reveal examples of narrative, elegiac, religious, and epic poetry. This wealth of literary type is unique to England during this early period. No other European country of this time had produced such a variety of poetry.

The Old English language. Most people have not read Old English verse in the original language because a speaker of modern English would not recognize most of the words. The language has changed greatly. The language before Alfred's reign was spelled in a phonetic imitation of the speech. Most of the examples of Old English existing today were preserved by scribes. The scribes were usually monks who used many Latin forms and spellings when writing the Saxon language.

During the reign of Alfred, spelling became more regular. By the time of Aelfric the spelling of West Saxon became standardized. The Anglo-Saxon language is of Germanic origin. Germanic is an Indo-European language. Other Germanic languages of the time are Old Saxon, Old Frisian, Old Norse, and Old High German.

Most of the Anglo-Saxon (Old English) words that remain are basic parts of the modern English vocabulary. Such words as father (*faeder*), mother (*moder*), friend (*freond*), sheep (*sceap*), and heaven (*heafon*) are of Anglo-Saxon origin. Prepositions and conjunctions, as well as most pronouns, articles, and auxiliary verbs, come from the Anglo-Saxon. Although the actual number of Anglo-Saxon words retained in modern English may be outweighed by those from other languages, these Anglo-Saxon words are used more frequently in normal sentences. Anglo-Saxon depended upon *inflections* to indicate gender and grammatical function. The chart shows the inflectional structure of pronouns.

		First	Second	Third: Masculine	Feminine	Neuter
Singular	**Nom.**	ic	ðū	hē	hēo	hit
	Gen.	mîn	ðîn	his	hiere	his
	Dat.	mē	ðē	him	hiere	him
	Acc.	mec, mē	ðec ðē	hine	hîe	hit
Plural	**Nom.**	wē	gē		hîe	
	Gen.	ūnser, ūre	ēower		hiera	
	Dat.	ūs	ēow		him	
	Acc.	ūsic, ūs	ēowic		hîe	

Nouns, pronouns, adjectives, adverbs, verbs, and even the article *the* were all inflected. As the chart illustrates, the pronouns in modern English can be traced to Anglo-Saxon. Some have undergone spelling changes. Others, such as *me, we, he, us, his,* or *him* have retained their original forms.

➤ Complete this activity.

1.17   a. Study the Anglo-Saxon passage carefully.

        b. Locate any words that are spelled or pronounced nearly as they are today.

> (1) And eft hē ongan hī æt þǣre sǣ lǣran. And him
> wæs mycel menegu tō gegaderod, swā þæt hē on scip
> ēode, and on þǣre sǣ wæs; and eall sēo menegu ymbe
> þā sǣ wæs on lande. (2) And hē hi fela on begspellum
> lǣrde, and him tō cwæð on his lāre, (3) Gehȳrað:
> Ūt ēode sē sǣdere his sǣd tō sāwenne. (4) And þā hē
> seow, sum fēoll wið þone weg, and fugelas cōmon and
> hit frǣton. (5) Sum fēoll ofer stānscyligean, þǣr hit
> næfde mycele eorðan, and sōna ūp ēode; and for þām hit
> næfde eorðan þiccnesse, (6) þā hit ūp ēode, sēo sunne
> hit forswǣlde, and hit forscranc, for þām hit wyrtruman
> næfde. (7) And sum fēoll on þornas; þā stigon ðā
> þornas and forðrysmodon þæt, and hit wæstm ne bær.
> (8) And sum fēoll on gōd land, and hit sealde *ūppstīg-*
> *endne* and *wexendne* wæstm; and ān brōhte þritig-
> fealdne, sum syxtigfealdne, sum hundfealdne.[1]

        c. List the words you recognize here. List each word only once. Use *modern* English spelling.

_____

_____

_____

_____

_____

_____

_____

        d. Now read Mark 4:1-8 and compare the two.

➤ Answer these questions.

1.18   Why do we have so few examples of Anglo-Saxon literature? _____

_____

_____

1.19   What is Old English? _____

_____

_____

_____

[1]*Bright's Anglo-Saxon Reader*, revised and enlarged by James R. Hulbert (New York: Holt, Rinehart, and Winston, 1935), p. 1.

The poet and oral tradition. The poet was a highly respected member of early society. He could come from many backgrounds—priest, historian, and entertainer. He recorded the rituals, accomplishments, and beliefs of his culture. He was the bearer and the preserver of tradition. The most accurate historical accounts of early Anglo-Saxon times are poetic.

Often called a *scop*, the poet told older stories and embellished them, or changed them. Although the poet knew his material well, he always varied it in one way or another. The Anglo-Saxon *scop*, or poet, used certain set formulas to relate a new tale or to adapt an old one. In the oral tradition each telling differed from the last.

Since a poet often told or sang his story without interruption, he had to have certain frameworks and patterns with which to improvise. Part of this structure included the use of certain **alliterative** and rhythmical patterns as well as poetic idioms. Because alliteration and rhythm are aids to memory, the poet could draw upon various formulas to express common ideas. By utilizing his storehouse of automatic phrases whenever possible, the poet could quickly compose the next line. A poet had to think quickly and to be skilled in language. The oral tradition of poetry contributed an unmatched richness of expression.

Anglo-Saxon rhythm depends upon a combination of weak and heavy stresses in many combinations. The basic unit of meter in Anglo-Saxon verse is the half-line. Each half-line is made up of a phrase with two stresses. A line of Anglo-Saxon poetry consists of two half-lines separated by a pause or break, joined together by alliteration. An Anglo-Saxon line of poetry may vary in length, ranging from eight syllables to about twenty syllables. Whatever the length, each line consists of four stresses, two in each halfline. The initial letter of one or more stressed words in the first half-line must alliterate with the initial letter in the first stress of the second half-line.

In the following example notice the half-line break, called a **caesura**, the stresses (´ ´) and the alliteration (_).

```
       Oft Scyld Scēfing          sceaþena þrēatum,
  5    monegum mǣgpum             mēodosetla oftēah,
       egsode eorl[as],           syððan ǣrest wearð
       fēasceaft funden;          hē þæs frōfre gebād,
       wēox under wolcnum         weorðmyndum þāh,
       oð þæt him ǣghwylc         ymbsittendra
 10    ofer hrónrāde              hȳran scólde,
       gómban gyldan              þæt wæs gōd cyning!
```

Anglo-Saxon poetic language is rich in metaphor. A frequently used device is a double metaphor, or **kenning**. The kenning is a form of expression unfamiliar to most speakers of modern English. This compounding of words and ideas is refreshing when used skillfully. Several kennings exist for the sea. Two of the most common sea kennings are "whaleroad" (*hron-rade*) and "swanroad" (*swan-race*), Kennings can refer to almost anything in nature or life. The sun was referred to as the "world-candle" (*woruldcandel*), the speech of a man is often called his "wordhoard" (*wordhord*), and a wanderer is called an "earth-stepper" (*eardstapa*).

Define these words. Use a dictionary if necessary.

1.20   *scop* _____

        _____

1.21   Old English meter_____

        _____

[2]Howell D. Chickering, Jr., *Beowulf: A Dual-Language Edition* (New York: Anchor Books, 1977), p. 48.

1.22   alliteration _____

_____

1.23   kenning _____

_____

Complete this activity.

1.24   Write some kennings of your own. Show them to a friend or classmate. Can he or she identify the meaning?

Adult Check   _____
                   Initial   Date

The epic and Beowulf. One great Anglo-Saxon epic has survived intact—*Beowulf.* The word *epic* comes from the Greek word meaning *tale*. An epic is a long narrative poem dealing with heroic characters and heroic actions. The theme of an epic deals with universal qualities. The narrative is composed from a nation's or a people's history; it is national in scope. The hero is an ideal person of almost superhuman qualities. He is loyal to his country or people, brave, strong, and shrewd. The style of the epic is elevated and dignified. Most epics start *in medias res*, in the middle of the story. The narrator then explains previous action as the story progresses.

Beowulf is a long narrative poem that can be divided into two main sections. The first section deals with the young noble Beowulf who leads his men to Hrothgar's kingdom and offers to rid the Danes of a terrible monster, Grendel. The second section deals with the elder King Beowulf who has served his people well and who goes out to fight a fiery dragon that is plaguing the kingdom, knowing that this battle will be his last.

Beowulf reveals many of the customs and ideals of Anglo-Saxon culture. To understand the poem, some of these customs and ideals must be studied. The **comitatus** relationship between the *Hlaford* (lord) and his *witan* (council or retainers) was one of the most important in Anglo-Saxon culture. The lord protected his retainers, saw to their needs, paid their debts, and settled their disputes. The retainers, in return, pledged their loyalty and support to the lord at all times, especially in times of need or of war.

To be abandoned by the lord or dismissed because of a lack of loyalty was banishment for a retainer. Other lords would not accept lone retainers readily. The death of a lord was tragic if he had no successor because all of his retainers became detached from any comitatus relationship and could not easily find a new lord. This lonely relationship was the plight of the poet in "The Wanderer."

In *Beowulf* this relationship is seen between Hrothgar and his retainers and between Beowulf and his men. The comitatus also extended to a longstanding bond between the Geats (Beowulf's people) and the Danes (Hrothgar's people). Because of this bond, Beowulf and his men left their homes and traveled to the land of the Danes to help them in time of need. The breakdown of comitatus is also seen in Beowulf. Near the end of the poem, Beowulf and his retainers went out to fight the fiery dragon that had been plaguing the kingdom. All the retainers, except one, became frightened and ran off to hide in the woods.

The one supporter, Wiglaf, remained with Beowulf to the end. Because of his loyalty, Wiglaf was named successor by the dying Beowulf. Because of their desertion, the other retainers were disgraced. Their cowardice was announced so that no other lord would accept them. They and their families had to seek new dwellings.

Another element of Anglo-Saxon culture that must be understood is the attitude toward fame. Fame in this case was identified with a good name that would live on after a man's death. A man lived his life so that his good name and his brave deeds might live on forever. Any man disgraced by or disloyal to his lord would not achieve fame.

This attitude toward fame was closely linked to the Anglo-Saxon attitude toward life itself. Life was looked upon as transitory, as passing quickly. The harshness of the weather, as well as the ravages of war and illness, were constant reminders of this fleeting nature of man's life.

Both fame and the transitory nature of life were linked to the comitatus. The relationship of the comitatus could ease the burdens of a hard life. The lord, also called the ring-giver, would bestow treasure on his retainers, would provide food and shelter in time of peace, and would generally make life more bearable.

Christianity played an important role in Anglo-Saxon culture and in *Beowulf*. Early Christianity was a blending of two systems, the Germanic and the Christian. Many ancient Germanic customs were retained, but were given Christian purpose. In *Beowulf*, for example, both God and Wyrd (Fate) are addressed. Each, however, has a place. God is always superior to Wyrd in the poem.

The burials mentioned in *Beowulf*, that of Sculd Scefing in the beginning and of Beowulf at the end, were traditional Anglo-Saxon or Viking burials. In *Beowulf* they were neither pagan nor Christian in themselves. They were in keeping with the cultural traditions of the people.

Such burials discovered in this century by archaeologists have revealed several Christian artifacts among the treasures buried with the body. Many of the descriptions of swords, helmets, goblets, and other artifacts found in Beowulf correspond to those artifacts found by archaeologists at Sutton Hoo in 1939 and at other burial sites.

Complete these statements.

1.25 The relationship that existed between the lord and his retainers was known as _____ .

1.26 To the Anglo-Saxon, fame meant _____ .

1.27 The hero in an epic is _____ .

1.28 Archaeologists have uncovered _____ in this century that date back to the Anglo-Saxon period.

1.29 A famous ship burial discovered in England in 1939 was _____ .

The extant manuscript dates from the year A.D. 1000, but *Beowulf* was written at least two hundred years before that time. Other copies must have existed, but Viking raids most likely destroyed them. The poem mentions a specific historical event: Hygelac, a Geat, was killed in a raid on the Frisians. This fact was validated by Gregory of Tours, a historian who recorded the date of Hygelac's death as A.D. 521.

A probable date for the writing of Beowulf would be during the time of Venerable Bede (A.D. 673–A.D. 735). The latest possible date would be the A.D. 790's to the 830's. The Danes had begun to overrun England by this time, and Anglo-Saxon feeling toward the Danes grew more hostile than the feelings exhibited in the poem. Like the *Illiad* and the *Odyssey*, Beowulf is a product of oral poetic tradition. The poem was probably copied from the song of a bard or scop. Perhaps the writer standardized some of the elements of the poem. No evidence can prove that one man could not have written it. All that can be ascertained is that *Beowulf* was based on the oral stories. The Beowulf poet was the recorder of the product of many storytellers.

The story was probably based on a folktale. The name *Beowulf* was not common for that Anglo-Saxon period.

Beowulf consists of 3,182 lines of unrhymed alliterative meter. It consists of an introduction and 43 fitts, or sections. The poem opens with the sea burial of Scyld Scefing who founded the Danish royal line. The first fifty lines cite Scyld Scefing's lifetime accomplishments. The funeral was a poetic variation of Viking royal ship burial similar to the burial finds at Sutton Hoo and Oseburg, Norway. Like Scyld Beowulf came over the water, strong and courageous, aiding the Danes.

The main story begins in Denmark with the problems of King Hrothgar. The monster Grendel invades the Hall, called Heorot, by night and devours Hrothgar's retainer. Beowulf, who is prince of the Geats, a people inhabiting the southern part of Sweden, arrives with his men to rid Hrothgar of this monster. After a feast and entertainment in the hall, Beowulf begins his watch while his men sleep.

710
x1

Then up from the marsh,   under misty cliffs,
Grendel came walking;   he bore God's wrath.
The evil thief planned   to trap some human,
one of man's kind,   in the towering hall.
Under dark skies   he came till he saw

715
the shining wine-hall,   house of gold-giving,
a joy to men,   plated high with gold.
It was not the first time   he had visited Hrothgar;
never in his life,   before or after,
did he find harder luck   or retainers in hall.

720 The evil warrior,   deprived of joys,
     came up to the building;   the door burst open,
     though bound with iron,   as soon as he touched it,
     huge in his blood-lust;   enraged, he ripped open
     the mouth of the hall;   quickly rushed in—
725 the monster stepped   on the bright-paved floor,
     crazed with evil anger;   from his strange eyes
     an ugly light   shone out like fire.
     There in the hall   he saw many men—
     the band of kinsmen   all sleeping together,
730 a troop of young warriors.   Then his heart laughed;
     evil monster,   he thought he would take
     the life from each body,   eat them all
     before day came;   the gluttonous thought
     of a full-bellied feast   was hot upon him.
735 No longer his fate   to feed on mankind,
     after that night.   The mighty man,
     kinsman of Hygelac,   watched how the killer
     would want to move   in sudden attack.
     Nor did the monster   think long to delay:
740 he lunged the next moment,   seized a warrior,
     gutted him sleeping   —ripped him apart—
     bit into muscles,   swilled blood from veins,
     tore off gobbets,   in hardly a moment
     had eaten him up,   all of the dead man,
745 even hands and feet.   He stepped further in,
     and caught in his claws   the strong-minded man
     where he lay on his bed—   the evil assailant
     snatched at him, clutching;   hand met claw,
     he sat straight at once,   thrust the arm back.
750 The shepherd of sins   then instantly knew
     he had never encountered,   in any region
     of this middle-earth,   in any other man,
     a stronger hand-grip;   at heart he feared
     for his wretched life,   but he could not move.
755 He wanted escape,   to flee to the fen,
     join the devils' rout.   Such greeting in hall
     he had never met   before in his life.
     Then the brave man remembered,   kinsman of Hygelac
     his speeches that evening,   rose to his feet
760 and held him close;   fingers snapped;
     the giant pulled away,   the noble moved with him.
     The ill-famed creature   thought to go elsewhere,
     anywhere possible,   away from the hall,
     into deep marshes,   felt his fingers
765 in a terrible grip.   An unhappy journey
     the evil harmer   had made to Heorot.
     The king's hall thundered: to all the Danes,
     the city's inhabitants,   to every brave listener
     it was a wild mead-sharing.   The grapplers were furious
770 angry hall-guards.   The building clattered;
     it was a great wonder   the mead-hall withstood
     those two battle-ragers,   did not crash to earth,
     tall-standing house.   But inside and out
     good smiths had turned   strong iron bands,

13

775 made the walls fast.   Many mead-benches
inlaid with gold,   came up from the floor,
so I have heard,   where the fighters crashed.
Before this the wise men,   Scylding counselors,
had not expected   that any warrior
780 could ever destroy it,   splendid, horn-bright,
by ordinary means,   pull it down by craft,
unless licking fire   should swallow it in flames.
A sound went out,   loud and high,
raised horrible fear   in Danish hearts,
785 in each of the men   on the palisade wall
who heard the cry—   God's enemy
screaming his hate-song,   a victory-less tune,
the hellish captive   moaning his pain.
He held him tight,   the strongest man
790 who ever lived   in the days of this life.
XII The protector of nobles   had no desire
to let the killer-guest   walk away free,
nor thought his life   could do the least service
to any nation.   Beowulf's warriors
795 all drew their swords,   time-tested heirlooms,
wanted to defend   the life of their comrade,
their famous chief,   however they could.
But they did not know,   as they entered the fight,
hard-minded men,   battle-warriors,
800 meaning to swing   from every side,
to cut out his soul,   that keen battle-edges,
best iron in the world,   sharpest blade,
could not harm him,   the evil demon,
not touch him at all —   he had bespelled
805 all weapons of battle.   His leave-taking,
his life's parting   from the days of this world
was to be painful;   the alien spirit
was to journey far   in the power of fiends.
Then he discovered,   who earlier brought
810 trouble of heart   to the race of men
by his many crimes   —at feud with God—
that his body-casing   would not keep life:
that Hygelac's kinsman,   the bold-hearted man,
had him in hand.   It was hateful to each
815 that the other lived.   The terrible creature
took a body wound there;   a gaping tear
opened in his shoulder;   tendons popped,
muscle slipped the bone.   Glory in battle
was given to Beowulf;   Grendel fled,
820 wounded, death-sick,   under marshy hills
to his joyless den;   with that huge wound
he knew for certain   his life had ended,
the sum of his days.   The desire of all Danes
had come to pass in   that deadly fight.[3]

[3]Beowulf, pp. 89, 91, 93, 95, 97.

Answer *true* or *false*.

1.30 _____ In this section of Beowulf, no one is killed.

1.31 _____ Grendel burst through iron-bound doors.

1.32 _____ Heorot is the king of the Danes.

1.33 _____ Beowulf fought Grendel with a sword.

1.34 _____ Grendel fled the hall and returned to his den.

1.35 _____ Grendel lost his arm in the fight.

Grendel returns to his lair to die. Beowulf has emerged victorious. The claw of the monster is displayed over the door of the meadhall.

The next morning all the warriors come to the hall to see the evidence of Grendel's defeat. That night a banquet is given in honor of Beowulf. At the banquet the queen, Wealhtheow, enters and speaks to Beowulf.

> [Then Wealhtheow spoke:]
> "Accept this cup,   my noble lord,
> 1170 gold-giving king;   be filled in your joys,
> treasure-friend to all,   and give to the Geats
> your kind words,   as is proper for men;
> in your generous mind,   be gracious to the Weders,
> remembering the gifts   you have from all tribes.
> 1175 I have been told   you would have this warrior
> for your son.   Heorot is cleansed,
> bright hall of rings;   use while you may
> your gifts from so many,   and leave to your kinsmen
> the nation and folk   when you must go forth
> 1180 to await your judgment.   Full well I know
> of my gracious Hrothulf   that he would rule
> the young men in honor,   would keep all well,
> if you should give up   this world before him.
> I expect he will want   to repay our sons
> 1185 only with good   once he recalls
> all we have done   when he was younger
> to honor his desires   and his name in the world."[4]

As the banquet progresses, the scop sings about a tragic feud from the past. This song foreshadows the impending fall of the Danish royalty.

After all have retired for the night, Grendel's mother invades the hall where many visiting nobles are sleeping. She quickly snatches up a chieftain and carries him off to her lair.

Beowulf starts after the monster's mother. Hrothgar has again appealed to Beowulf and has promised to reward him with treasure. Beowulf tracks Grendel's mother to her lair—a *mere*, or lake. The battle is fierce and Beowulf is unable to wound the monster until he finds a mighty sword. He kills the monster, bringing to an end the evil reign of terror.

When Hrothgar hears of Beowulf's victory he is pleased. In an eloquent sermon he warns Beowulf about the dangers of pride. Beowulf leaves the next day, after receiving the gifts of the king.

Beowulf relates his adventures to his uncle, King Hygelac, when he returns to his home and bestows his treasures upon his king. In return Beowulf is granted land and gifts.

[4]Beowulf, p. 117.

Match these items.

1.36 _____ Wealhtheow   a. Hrothgar's hall

1.37 _____ Heorot   b. Beowulf's sword

1.38 _____ Grendel's mother   c. king of the Danes

1.39 _____ Hygelac   d. Hrothgar's queen

1.40 _____ Hrothgar   e. king of the Geats

                                                             f. carried off a chieftain

A space of about fifty years passes. Beowulf is king for most of this time. The tale resumes in Beowulf's old age. A dragon has dwelt in the kingdom for years guarding a treasure. One day, a cup is stolen from the treasure, and the dragon begins his revenge on Beowulf's kingdom. Beowulf must fight the dragon and protect his people. He calls his retainers to assist him, but knows that ultimately he must fight the dragon alone.

The dragon's fiery breath burns Beowulf, causing his men to desert him. Only one warrior, Wiglaf, comes to Beowulf's aid. As the dragon attacks again, Beowulf breaks his sword on the dragon's head. The dragon wounds Beowulf. Wiglaf again comes to his aid. Although Beowulf kills the dragon, he has sustained a fatal wound.

Beowulf asks Wiglaf to bring the treasure for him to see before he dies.

>   [Beowulf spoke,]
> old in his grief,   as he saw the gold:
> "I give thanks aloud   to the Lord of all,
> 2795   King of glories,   eternal Ruler,
> for the bright treasures   I can see here,
> that I might have gained   such gifts as these
> for the sake of my people   before I died.
> Now that I have given   my old life-span
> 2800   for this heap of treasures,   you are to watch
> the country's needs.   I can stay no longer.
> Order a bright mound   made by the brave,
> after the pyre,   at the sea's edge;
> let it rise high on   Whale's Cliff,
> 2805   a memorial to my people,   that ever after
> sailors will call it   'Beowulf's barrow'
> when the steep ships drive   out on the sea,
> on the darkness of waters,   from lands far away."
> From round his throat   he took the golden collar,
> 2810   brave-hearted king,   and gave to his thane,
> the young spearfighter,   his gold-plated helmet,
> rings, mail-shirt,   bade use them well:
> "You are the last   man of our tribe,
> the race of Wægmundings;   fate has swept
> 2815   all my kinsmen   to their final doom,
> undaunted nobles.   I must follow them."
> That was the last word   of the old man
> from the thoughts of his heart   before he chose
> the high battle-flames;   out from his breast
> 2820   his soul went to seek   the doom of the just.[5]

---

[5]Beowulf, pp. 217, 19.

Beowulf's conscience is clear. He specifies his funeral requests, then dies. Wiglaf mourns Beowulf's death. When the troops return, Wiglaf speaks severely to the men who have disgraced the *comitatus* and condemns them to a life of wandering.

The king's council is notified of Beowulf's death. The people realize that their courageous protector has left them at the mercy of their enemies. The poem ends with Beowulf's funeral. His body is placed on a funeral pyre by the sea with the treasures from the cave. After the fire has consumed the body, both ashes and remaining treasures are buried near the sea.

The poem closes with an epitaph.

3180   They said that he was,   of the kings of this world,
   the kindest to his men,   the most courteous man.
   the best to his people,   and most eager for fame.[6]

Beowulf is essentially a Christian poem. The rites of burial and the references to Wyrd reflect the pagan background of the Anglo-Saxon, but are blended skillfully with Christian custom and ideals of the time. Direct Biblical references are to the Old Testament—to Creation, the Flood, and Cain.

Beowulf sought God's will in his fights with Grendel and the dragon. Hrothgar praised and thanked God for Beowulf's victory. Christian diction and Christian ideals are found throughout the poem.

The secular side of Anglo-Saxon society is also found in Beowulf more than any other Anglo-Saxon poem. The poem is proving to reflect an accurate accounting of some of the artifacts, ornaments, and architecture of the time.

[6]Beowulf, p. 243

The discovery of gold treasures and artifacts at Sutton Hoo verifies the existence of golden armor and ornaments such as those described in *Beowulf*. It also verifies as authentic some of the customs of the time. Two helmets decorated with a boar image have been discovered in England—one at Sutton Hoo and one at Bently Grange. These helmets probably date back to the sixth century. A small lyre was also found. Anglo-Saxon decorations depended upon the contrast of light and dark. Jewels were used to contrast with metal. Patterns were similar to the Celtic in part with pierced patterns and interlaced designs.

In *Beowulf* the description of Hrothgar's hall is the only record of an early Anglo-Saxon building. This hall was constructed of timber strengthened with iron bands. The floors were wooden, stone, or possibly even tile. The hall was used for eating, for sleeping, for meetings, and for entertainment. It was usually surrounded by houses. Houses of the Anglo-Saxon period were rectangular in shape with columns or external beams supporting the roof. They were constructed of wattle and daub or of stone and earth.

Beowulf is a moving epic and proves that the Anglo-Saxons were an intelligent, sensitive, and artistic people. Recent discoveries are bearing out this evidence and making historians and the people at large reexamine what was once considered a barbarian age of primitive people.

Match the following term with its correct answer.

1.41	_____ Wyrd	a.	a lake or pool
1.42	_____ epic	b.	Beowulf's uncle
1.43	_____ *in medias res*	c.	people of southern Sweden
1.44	_____ Geats	d.	Hrothgar's queen
1.45	_____ Grendel	e.	fate
1.46	_____ Wealhtheow	f.	loyal companion of Beowulf
1.47	_____ mere	g.	a long narrative poem about national heroes
1.48	_____ Hygelac	h.	a monster
1.49	_____ Wiglaf	i.	the meadhall
		j.	in the middle of things
		k.	the poet

Complete this activity.

1.50 Choose one of these activities to complete outside of class.

a. Visit a nearby library. Research one of the following topics:

Sutton Hoo
Anglo-Saxon England

b. Find a translation of Beowulf, read it, and write your impressions.

c. Write a short paper based on the Beowulf epic. Using a more modern hero, create your own epic. You may want to limit your paper to one episode. Remember to adjust your language to fit your subject.

Adult Check _____
Initial   Date

18

The elegy. An elegy is a formal poem, a poet's meditation upon a serious subject. "Widsith" is an elegy about the life of a minstrel who traveled as he told many stories about heroes and events. "Widsith" is probably the oldest poem in English. Dating back to the seventh century, it describes over fifty tribes and nearly as many heroes who lived in England after the third century. The poem, set in pre-Anglo-Saxon times, seems to have been a serious attempt to relate the heroes and the events that were important to the Britons. Some of these people referred to in the poem were famous in Gothic history and reappeared in the German poetry of the late medieval period.

Early English society depended upon numbers for survival. Men banded together for companionship and protection. A man sought the protection of a lord. For this reason an exile was one of the most lonely and vulnerable of men. Exiles were the main characters of most old English elegies. Both "The Wanderer" and "The Seafarer" are elegiac monologues concerning themselves with questions about salvation.

The wanderer in the first part of the poem was searching for a new lord because his lord had died. The next part of the poem is a flashback to the meadhall and the times of former happiness. The poet lamented the loss of his friend and lord and the loss of his whole way of life. The poet said that a wise man should not boast of future accomplishments until he knows more about himself. He described the emptiness of earthly glory, the finiteness of man's earthly life. The poet ended by saying that it is good to seek God's forgiveness and to keep the faith.

THE WANDERER

[*The Wanderer* is an elegy uttered by one who had formerly known happiness and honour in his lord's hall. Now his lord is dead, and he has lost his post. He has become a wanderer who knows that 'sorrow's crown of sorrow is remembering happier things.']

OFTEN the solitary man prays for favour, for the mercy of the Lord, though, sad at heart, he must needs stir with his hands for a weary while the icy sea across the watery ways, must journey the paths of exile; settled in truth is fate! So spoke the wanderer, mindful of hardships, of cruel slaughters, of the fall of kinsmen:

'Often I must bewail my sorrows in my loneliness at the dawn of each day; there is none of living men now to whom I dare speak my heart openly. I know for a truth that it is a noble custom for a man to bind fast the thoughts of his heart, to treasure his broodings, let him think as he will. Nor can the weary in mood resist fate, nor does the fierce thought avail anything. Wherefore those eager for glory often bind fast in their secret hearts a sad thought. So I, sundered from my native land, far from noble kinsmen, often sad at heart, had to fetter my mind, when in years gone by the darkness of the earth covered my gold-friend, and I went thence in wretchedness with wintry care upon me over the frozen waves, gloomily sought the hall of a treasure-giver wherever I could find him far or near, who might know me in the mead hall or comfort me, left without friends, treat me with kindness. He knows who puts it to the test how cruel a comrade is sorrow for him who has few dear protectors; his is the path of exile, in no wise the twisted gold; a chill body, in no wise the riches of the earth; he thinks of retainers in hall and the receiving of treasure, of how in his youth his gold-friend was kind to him at the feast. The joy has perished. Wherefore he knows this who must long forgo the counsels of his dear lord and friend, when sorrow and sleep together often bind the poor solitary man; it seems to him in his mind that he clasps and kisses his lord and lays hands and head on his knee, as when erstwhile in past days he was near the giftthrone; then the friendless man wakes again, sees before him the dark waves, the seabirds bathing, spreading their feathers; frost and snow falling mingled with hail. Then heavier are the wounds in his heart, sore for his beloved; sorrow is renewed. Then the memory of kinsmen crosses his mind; he greets them with songs; he gazes on them eagerly. The companions of warriors swim away again; the souls of sailors bring there not many known songs. Care is renewed in him who

19

must needs send very often his weary mind over the frozen waves. And thus I cannot think why in this world my mind becomes not overcast when I consider all the life of earls, how of a sudden they have given up hall, courageous retainers. So this world each day passes and falls; for a man cannot become wise till he has his share of years in the world. A wise man must be patient, not over-passionate, nor over-hasty of speech, nor over-weak or rash in war, nor over-fearful, nor over-glad, nor over-covetous, never over-eager to boast ere he has full knowledge. A man must bide his time, when he boasts in his speech, until he knows well in his pride whither the thoughts of the mind will turn. A wise man must see how dreary it will be when all the riches of this world stand waste, as in different places throughout this world walls stand, blown upon by winds, hung with frost, the dwellings in ruins. The wine halls crumble; the rulers lie low, bereft of joy; the mighty warriors have all fallen in their pride by the wall; war carried off some, bore them on far paths; one the raven bore away over the high sea; one the grey wolf gave over to death; one an earl with sad face hid in the earth-cave. Thus did the creator of men lay waste this earth till the old work of giants stood empty, free from the revel of castle-dwellers. Then he who has thought wisely of the foundation of things and who deeply ponders this dark life, wise in his heart, often turns his thoughts to the many slaughters of the past and speaks these words:

"'Whither has gone the horse? Whither has gone the man? Whither has gone the giver of treasure? Whither has gone the place of feasting? Where are the joys of hail? Alas, the bright cup! Alas, the warrior in his corslet! Alas, the glory of the prince! How that time has passed away, has grown dark under the shadow of night, as if it had never been! Now in the place of the dear warriors stands a wall, wondrous high, covered with serpent shapes; the might of the ash-wood spears has carried off the earls, the weapon greedy for slaughter—a glorious fate; and storms beat upon these rocky slopes; the falling storm binds the earth, the terror of winter. Then comes darkness, the night shadow casts gloom, sends from the north fierce hailstorms to the terror of men. Everything is full of hardship in the kingdom of earth; the decree of fate changes the world under the heavens. Here possessions are transient, here friends are transient, here man is transient, here woman is transient; all this firm-set earth becomes empty."

So spoke the wise man in his heart, and sat apart in thought. Good is he who holds his faith; nor shall a man ever show forth too quickly the sorrow of his breast, except he, the earl, first know how to work its cure bravely. Well is it for him who seeks mercy, comfort from the Father in heaven, where for us all security stands.

→ **Reread this prose translation of "The Wanderer."** Answer the following questions based on this translation.

1.51 What did the poet say the wise man must be?

a. _____

b. _____

c. _____

d. _____

e. _____

f. _____

g. _____

[7]From *Anglo-Saxon Poetry*, selected and translated by R. K. Gordon. An Everyman's Library Edition. Reprinted by permission of the publisher in the United States, E. P. Dutton, *and world rights by J. M. Dent, London, pp. 73-75.

1.52 What must the wise man come to realize? _____

_____

_____

1.53 How does the description of a wise man reflect Christian attitudes? _____

_____

_____

_____

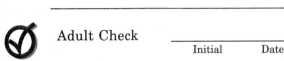 Adult Check _____
                           Initial   Date

The sea is a theme used in English literature from earliest times. The *Exeter Book* contains the "Seafarer." Other works about the sea include those by Cynewulf and the Biblical accounts of the Flood and the parting of the Red Sea.

Written in the fifth or sixth century, "The Seafarer" deals with the perils and adventures of a sailor's life. Such hazards as loneliness and storms are weighed against the excitement and freedom of a life at sea.

"The Seafarer" is composed in the form of a soliloquy. The old sailor told about all the hard times he had experienced at sea. He expressed doubts about his impending journey. Then the poet explained the mortality of humans saying that fame can be accomplished by working against the devil. The poem ends with the idea of the futility of life, especially the life of a sinner.

THE SEAFARER

[*The Seafarer* is taken by some critics to be a dialogue in which an old sailor tells of the lonely sufferings of life at sea, and is answered by a youth who urges that it is the hardness of the life which makes it attractive. The poem, however, may be a monologue in which the speaker tells of his sufferings, but also admits the fascination of the sea. The mood of contempt for the luxuries of land and his yearning to set forth on the voyage lead him to think of the future life and the fleeting nature of earthly pomps and joys.]

I CAN utter a true song about myself, tell of my travels, how in toilsome days I often suffered a time of hardship, how I have borne bitter sorrow in my breast, made trial of many sorrowful abodes on ships; dread was the rolling of the waves. There the hard night-watch at the boat's prow was often my task, when it tosses by the cliffs. Afflicted with cold, my feet were fettered by frost, by chill bonds. There my sorrows, hot round my heart, were sighed forth; hunger within rent the mind of the sea-weary man. The man who fares most prosperously on land knows not how I, careworn, have spent a winter as an exile on the ice-cold sea, cut off from kinsmen, hung round with icicles. The hail flew in showers. I heard naught there save the sea booming, the ice-cold billow, at times the song of the swan. I took my gladness in the cry of the gannet and the sound of the curlew instead of the laughter of men, in the screaming gull instead of the drink of mead. There storms beat upon the rocky cliffs; there the tern with icy feathers answered them; full often the dewy-winged eagle screamed around. No protector could comfort the heart in its need. And yet he who has the bliss of life, who, proud and flushed with wine, suffers few hardships in the city, little believes how I often in weariness had to dwell on the ocean path. The shadow of night grew dark, snow came from the north, frost bound the earth; hail fell on the ground, coldest of grain. And yet the thoughts of my heart are now stirred that I myself should make trial of the high streams, of the tossing of the salt waves; the desire of the heart always exhorts to venture forth that I may visit the land of strange people far hence. And yet there is no man on earth so proud, nor so generous of his gifts, nor so bold in youth, nor so daring in his deeds, nor with a lord so gracious unto him, that he has not always anxiety about his seafaring, as to what the Lord will bestow on him. His thoughts are not of the harp, nor of receiving rings, nor of delight in a woman, nor of joy in the world, nor of aught else save the rolling of the waves; but he who sets out on the waters ever feels longing. The groves put forth blossoms; cities grow beautiful; the fields are fair; the world revives; all these urge the heart of the eager-minded man to a journey, him who thus purposes to fare far on the ways of the flood. Likewise the cuckoo exhorts with sad voice; the harbinger of summer sings, bodes bitter sorrow to the heart. The man knows not, the prosperous being, what some of those endure who most widely pace the paths of exile. And yet my heart is now restless in my breast, my mind is with the sea-flood over the whale's domain; it fares widely over the face of the earth, comes again to me eager and unsatisfied; the lone-flier screams, resistlessly urges the heart to the whale-way over the stretch of seas.

Wherefore the joys of the Lord are more inspiring for me than this dead fleeting life on earth. I have no faith that earthly riches will abide for ever. Each one of three things is ever uncertain ere its time comes; illness or age or hostility will take life away from a man doomed and dying. Wherefore the praise of living men who shall speak after he is gone, the best of fame after death for every man, is that he should strive ere he must depart, work on earth with bold deeds against the malice of fiends, against the devil, so that the children of men may later exalt him and his praise live afterwards among the angels for ever and ever, the joy of life eternal, delight amid angels.

The days have departed, all the pomps of earth's kingdom; kings, or emperors, or givers of gold, are not as of yore when they wrought among themselves greatest deeds of glory, and lived in most lordly splendour. This host has all fallen, the delights have departed; weaklings live on and possess this world, enjoy it by their toil. Glory is laid low; the nobleness of the earth ages and withers, as now every man does throughout the world. Old age comes on him; his face grows pale; grey-haired he laments; he knows that his former friends, the sons of princes, have been laid in the earth. Then, when life leaves him, his body can neither taste sweetness, nor feel pain, nor stir a hand, nor ponder in thought. Though he will strew the grave with gold, bury his brother with various treasures beside dead kinsmen, that will not go with him. To the soul full of sins the gold which it hoards while it lives here gives no help in the face of God's wrath. Great is the fear of God, whereby the earth turns; He established the mighty plains, the face of the earth, and the sky above. Foolish is he who fears not his Lord; death comes to him unexpected. Blessed is he who lives humbly; mercy comes to him from heaven; God establishes that heart in him because he trusts in his strength.

One must check a violent mind and control it with firmness, and be trustworthy to men, pure in ways of life.

Every man should show moderation in love towards a friend and enmity towards a foe... Fate is more strong, God more mighty than any man's thought. Let us consider where we possess our home, and then think how we may come thither, and let us then also attempt to win there, to the eternal bliss, where life springs from God's love, joy in heaven. Thanks be for ever to the Holy One because He, the Prince of glory, the Lord everlasting, has honoured us. Amen.[8]

Complete these activities.

1.54   Find two kennings in this translation of "The Seafarer."

a. _____

b. _____

[8]Gordon. pp. 76-78.

22

1.55   Several vivid descriptions of the sea occur in this poem. Find your favorite, copy it below, and explain why it is your favorite.

_____

_____

_____

_____

_____

1.56   Several passages in the last half of this poem were written in the style of proverbs. Select one of these passages and find a parallel in the Bible.

_____

_____

_____

_____

_____

"The Ruin" is a poetic description of the remains of a Roman city in England. It must have been written sometime in the eighth century, some three hundred years after the Romans withdrew from England. The stone walls and deserted hot baths were described by the poet. The poem is only a fragment.

THE RUIN

[This elegy on a ruined city with its fallen walls and departed glory is taken by many to refer to the city of Bath. The text of the poem is unfortunately in a very imperfect condition and the meaning often uncertain, but the passionate regret with which it pictures the city,

'Where a multitude of men breathed joy and woe
Long ago,'

makes it one of the greatest of Old English poems.]

WONDROUS is this wall-stone; broken by fate, the castles have decayed; the work of giants is crumbling. Roofs are fallen, ruinous are the towers, despoiled and are the towers with their gates; frost is on their cement, broken are the roofs, cut away, fallen undermined by age. The grasp of the earth, stout grip of the ground, holds its mighty builders, who have perished and gone; till now a hundred generations of men have died. Often this wall, grey with lichen and stained with red, unmoved under storms, has survived kingdom after kingdom; its lofty gate has fallen. . . the bold in spirit bound the foundation of the wall wondrously together with wires. Bright were the castledwellings, many the bath-houses, lofty the host of pinnacles, great the tumult of men, many a mead hall full of the joys of men, till Fate the mighty overturned that. The wide walls fell; days of pestilence came; death swept away all the bravery of men; their fortresses became waste places; the city fell to ruin. The multitudes who might have built it anew lay dead on the earth. Wherefore these courts are in decay and these lofty gates; the woodwork of the roof is stripped of tiles; the place has sunk into ruin, levelled to the hills, where in times past many a man light of heart and bright with gold, adorned with splendours, proud and flushed with wine, shone in war trappings, gazed on treasure, on silver, on precious stones, on riches, on possessions, on costly gems, on this bright castle of the broad kingdom. Stone courts stood here; the stream with its great gush sprang forth hotly; the wall enclosed all within its bright bosom; there the baths were hot in its centre; that was spacious...[9]

[9]Gordon, p. 84.

Complete this activity.

1.57 Think of a ruin in or near your town. Could you describe it in such a way that all of the history, the life behind that ruin would be apparent to a reader? Try to do this. Show your finished piece to a friend or read it to your class.

 Adult Check _____
Initial   Date

The riddle and gnomic verse. Old English riddles describe the objects and animals common to the people of the time. People of today learn much about early England by reading these poems. Some of the subjects of riddles include a swan, the wind, and a sword. Some of these old English riddles contain the Latin theories about weather. Other riddles may have been influenced by the riddles written in Latin.

A MOTH ate words. That seemed to me a strange event, when I heard of that wonder, that the worm, a thief in the darkness, should devour the song of a man, a famed utterance and a thing founded by a strong man. The thievish visitant was no whit the wiser for swallowing the words. (1.58)

MY abode is not silent, nor I myself loud voiced; the Lord laid laws upon us, shaped our course together; I am swifter than he, stronger at times, he more laborious; sometimes I rest; he must needs run on. I ever dwell in him while I live: if we are parted death is my destiny. (1.59)

[The 'foe of the wood' is probably the iron of the ploughshare which in the form of an axe destroys the tree, or it may be the farmer who turns forest into ploughed land. The former life of the wooden part of the plough as a tree is recalled. The two 'cunning points' are the courter and the share.]

MY nose is downward; I go deep and dig into the ground; I move as the grey foe of the wood guides me, and my lord who goes stooping as guardian at my tail; he pushes me in the plain, bears and urges me, sows in my track. I hasten forth, brought from the grove, strongly bound, carried on the wagon, I have many wounds; on one side of me as I go there is green, and on the other my track is clear black. Driven through my back a cunning point hangs beneath; another on my head fixed and prone falls at the side, so that I tear with my teeth, if he who is my lord serves me rightly from behind. (1.60)

OFTEN I must war against the wave and fight against the wind; I contend against them combined, when, buried by the billows, I go to seek the earth; my native land is strange to me. If I grow motionless I am mighty in the conflict; if I succeed not in that they are stronger than I, and straight way with rending they put me to rout; they wish to carry off what I must keep safe. I foil them in that if my tail endures and if the stones are able to hold fast against me in my strength. Ask what is my name. (1.61)

THE sea fed me, the water-covering enveloped me, and waves covered me, footless, close to earth. Often I open my mouth to the flood; now some man will eat my flesh; he cares not for my covering, when with the point of a knife he tears off the skin from my side and afterwards quickly eats me uncooked also...[10] (1.62)

Answer the riddles by identifying the objects. List your answers in the same order as the riddles appear in the text.

1.58 _____   1.61 _____

1.59 _____   1.62 _____

1.60 _____

[10]Gordon, pp. 294, 295, 303, 307.

24

Gnomes are maxims in verse. They are pithy, succinct sayings. Some of these gnomes express proverbs; some set forth morals, vices, or stress virtues; others describe nature. The gnomes may be combined into groups, such as the Gnomic Verses of the *Exeter Book*, or they may appear briefly within other types of verse.

A man shall utter wisdom, write secrets, sing songs, merit praise, expound glory, be diligent daily. A good man is mindful of a good and tame horse, known and tried and round of hoof. No man acquires too much. Well shall one keep a friend in all ways; often a man passes by the village afar off where he knows he has no certain friend. Unfriended, unblest, a man takes wolves for companions, a dangerous beast; full often that companion rends him. There shall be terror of the grey wolf; a grave for the dead man. It is grieved by hunger; it goes not around that with lamentation; the grey wolf weeps not indeed for the slaughter, the killing of men, but ever wishes it greater. A bandage shall be bound round; vengeance shall be for the brave man. The bow shall be for the arrow; to both alike shall man be a companion. Treasure becomes another's; a man shall give gold; God may give goods to the rich and take them away again. A hall shall stand, grow old itself. A tree which lies low grows least. Trees shall spread out and faith increase; it springs up in the breast of the merciful. A false man and foolish, venomous and faithless, God cares not for him. The Lord created many things which came to be long ago, bade them be thus henceforth. For every man wise words are fitting, the song for the singer and wisdom for the man. As many men as there are in the world, so many thoughts are there; each has his own heart's longing; yet the less for him who knows many songs and can play the harp with his hands, he has the gift of his music which God has given him. Hapless is he who must needs live alone; fate has decreed that he shall dwell friendless; it were better for him had he a brother, that they both were the sons of one man, of an earl, if they both should attack a boar or bear; that is a very fierce beast. Ever shall these warriors bear their armour and sleep together; never shall one mar their peace by tale-bearing ere death part them. They two shall sit at the chessboard while their anger passes away; they forget the shaping of harsh destinies; they have sport at the board. The idle hand of the gamester is at leisure long enough when it casts the dice but seldom in the broad ship, unless it is running under sail. Weary shall he be who rows against the wind; full often one blames the timid with reproaches, so that he loses courage, draws his oar on board. Guile shall go with evil, skill with things fitting; thus is the die stolen. Often they bandy words before they turn their backs on one another. The resolute man is everywhere ready. Hostility has been among mankind even since the earth swallowed the blood of Abel. That was not the hatred of a day from which wicked drops of blood sprang far and wide, great evil to men, to many people pernicious hate. Cain slew his own brother whom death carried off; far and wide was it known then that lasting hate injured men, so citizens. They were busy with strife of weapons far and wide throughout the earth; they devised and tempered the harmful sword. The shield shall be ready, the dart on its shaft, the edge on the sword and point on the spear, courage in the brave man. Helmet shall be for the bold man, and ever the soul of the base man shall be a treasure most paltry.'[11]

> **Write** *true* **or** *false* **for each statement.**

1.63	_____	*Beowulf* is probably the oldest poem in English.
1.64	_____	"The Wanderer" expresses the idea that life is transient.
1.65	_____	"The Seafarer" says that sinful man's life is futile.
1.66	_____	"The Ruin" describes an old Norman castle.
1.67	_____	Gnomes are the subject of riddles.

[11]Gordon, pp. 312-13.

Review the material in this section in preparation for the Self Test. The Self Test will check your mastery of this particular section. The items missed on this Self Test will indicate specific areas where restudy is needed for mastery.

SELF TEST 1

Complete these statements (each answer, 3 points).

1.01   Five different groups of people who have influenced Anglo-Saxon England include:

a. _____

b. _____

c. _____

d. _____

e. _____

1.02   Old English depended upon a. _____ and b. _____ .

1.03   Another name for poet is _____ .

1.04   The repetition of initial sounds in two or more words is called _____ .

1.05   A double metaphor used in early Anglo-Saxon poetry is called a _____ .

1.06   *Beowulf* is considered a great Anglo-Saxon _____ .

1.07   Beowulf fights a monster named _____ .

Write *true* **or** *false* (each answer, 1 point).

1.08   _____   Early Britons mined tin and fashioned weapons and tools out of bronze.

1.09   _____   The Picts constructed Stonehenge, a primitive building of planking, using the first bronze hinges.

1.010   _____   King Arthur was supposed to have lived around A.D. 500.

1.011   _____   The comitatus was a church group.

1.012   _____   The Catholic Church greatly influenced education in the Anglo-Saxon period.

1.013   _____   Bede's *Historia Ecclesiastica* describes the change from a barbaric society to a civilized culture.

1.014   _____   The *Anglo-Saxon Chronicle* was established by King Arthur.

1.015   _____   The Vikings broke the Danelaw by looting monasteries.

1.016   _____   Pronouns are usually of Anglo-Saxon origin.

1.017   _____   *Beowulf* was written in A.D. 838.

Match the following terms with the correct answer (each answer, 2 points). You may use some answers more than once.

1.018 _____ "The Wanderer"   a. elegy

1.019 _____ *Beowulf*   b. riddle

1.020 _____ "The Anchor"   c. gnome

1.021 _____ "The Ruin"   d. epic

1.022 _____ "The Seafarer"   e. history

1.023 _____ *Anglo-Saxon Chronicle*

Define or explain these terms (each answer, 4 points).

1.024 alliteration _____

_____

_____

1.025 Danelaw_____

_____

_____

1.026 Scyid Schefing_____

_____

_____

1.027 Hrothgar _____

_____

_____

Answer these questions (each answer, 5 points).

1.028 What one thing in life was most important to Beowulf and why?_____

_____

_____

1.029 Why is an exile so pitied by Anglo-Saxons? _____

_____

1.030 What is considered the oldest English poem? _____

1.031 What comitatus relationships are shown in Beowulf?

    a. _____

    b. _____

    c. _____

    d. _____

II. MEDIEVAL ENGLAND

The period between A.D. 1066, the date of the Norman Conquest, and the fourteenth century, the age of Chaucer, was a time of change. It was a transitional period in English literature, containing the last works in Anglo-Saxon, many Latin works, some Anglo-Norman works, and the first works in Middle English, the language that finally emerged as Norman language and culture blended with English language and culture.

This period between 1066 and 1300 also saw the rise of feudalism, the increase of church influence and power, and the gradual emergence of trade, of towns, and of a middle class.

In this section, you will briefly review the historical changes. You will learn more about the influence of feudalism and the church. You will examine the changes brought about as towns and trade began to grow. Finally, you will look at some of the literary forms that were used at this time.

SECTION OBJECTIVES

Review these objectives. When you have completed this section, you should be able to:

6. Explain the impact of the Norman conquest upon Anglo-Saxon society, language, and literature.

7. Identify the importance of feudalism and the church as reflected by Chaucer's *Canterbury Tales*.

8. Describe the types of literature that dominated the transitional period between A.D. 1066 and 1300.

VOCABULARY

Study these words to enhance your learning success in this section.

demesne	investiture
feudalism	manorialism
fief	vassal
folk ballad	

ENGLISH HISTORY (1066-1300)

English history between A.D. 1066 and A.D. 1300 is often referred to as the High Middle Ages. This period reflects the changes that England underwent as a result of the Norman Conquest.

Norman Conquest. Edward "The Confessor" was the king of England from A.D. 1042 to A.D. 1066. During his reign, many decisions of government fell to the nobles, because King Edward concentrated on the church and on the building of Westminster Abbey. After his death, the throne was claimed by two men: William of Normandy, Edward's nephew, and Harold Godwinson, a Saxon earl. Although the English supported Harold's claim, William invaded England in A.D. 1066, defeated the Saxons, and established himself as king.

The Normans virtually took over the land and the government. William the Conqueror awarded half of England to his Norman nobles, keeping one-fifth for himself. He set up a council of advisors and converted the Anglo-Saxon *witan* into a Great Council. Positions on this council were awarded to many Norman nobles. He named a Norman archbishop of Canterbury. He prevented conspiracy by requiring every lord to recognize him as supreme ruler. He also compiled a list of holdings for eleventh-century England. This list, called the *Domesday Book*, insured that all property holders were known for tax collection purposes.

Early kings after William. William's son, William II, was a poor ruler. He was succeeded by his brother, Henry "Beauclerc" (good clerk). Henry was an educated man and began to grant certain rights to nobles. He secured the support of the church. By marrying a Saxon princess, he also gained peasant support. He set up a more effective legal system.

Sir Thomas Becket   King Henry II

Another period of struggle for power followed Henry's death. His grandson became King Henry II. He set up the forerunner of the modern grand jury. Common law based upon legal precedents began to be upheld. Henry II appointed his friend Thomas à Becket, archbishop of Canterbury. Becket resisted attempts by the king to gain control of the church and was assassinated in Canterbury cathedral by the king's men. Becket became known as a martyr—the "holy blissful martyr" whose shrine is the object of Chaucer's pilgrimage.

Henry's son, Richard the Lion-Hearted, took the throne in 1189. A popular king and a hero of many medieval tales, Richard spent much time on crusades or as a captive in prison. He lessened the hold of **feudalism** by allowing nobles and knights to pay money rather than giving personal service in war. Richard hired mercenaries, or professional soldiers, to fight.

King John followed Richard. John had religious, domestic, and foreign problems during his reign. John was an unpopular king. He lost most of the English possessions in France. He was forced to surrender to the pope's wishes and also was forced to sign the "Magna Carta" at Runnymede by his own nobles.

The increased power of the church under Henry III created an anticlerical attitude among the people. A domestic power dispute led to the assembly of an informal parliament.

Edward I was king at the turn of the fourteenth century. He called the "model parliament" to win support for wars against Scotland and Wales. He conquered Wales, but could not defeat the Scots. He created a stronger monarchy, brought about a strong government ruled by king and Parliament and based on the principles of common law.

Match these names with the correct answer.

2.1 _____ William

2.2 _____ *Domesday Book*

2.3 _____ Thomas à Becket

2.4 _____ Harold

2.5 _____ King John

2.6 _____ Henry II

2.7 _____ Edward I

2.8 _____ Henry I

a. lost the throne to William

b. conquered Wales

c. the archbishop of Canterbury

d. the "Conqueror"

e. lost most English possessions in France

f. written by Geoffrey Chaucer

g. called "Beauclerc"

h. a list of property holders

i. set up the forerunner of the modern grand jury

Feudalism and manorialism. With the Normans came certain political, social, and economic systems. These systems were unlike the Anglo-Saxon systems and had been developing on the continent since the establishment of the Frankish kingdoms after the death of Charlemagne in the year A.D. 814. The political system was known as feudalism. The social and economic system was called **manorialism**.

Feudalism differed from one country to the next, but the basic concept remained the same. In the feudal system the king held a great deal of land. To insure loyalty and military support, he would grant parcels of land, known as **fiefs**, to church leaders and to nobles. This fief was granted in a ceremony of **investiture** at which the noble receiving the land became a **vassal** of the king and swore an oath of loyalty. Each noble, in turn, could grant fiefs to lesser nobles. These lesser nobles became vassals of the nobles. The lesser nobles, finally, could grant fiefs to knights. The knights then became vassals of the lesser noble. In time of war or of need in the kingdom each vassal was pledged to support his lord. Thus, the king could demand aid from the nobles, who in turn demanded aid from the lesser nobles. The lesser nobles demanded aid from the knights. The king had at his command all the nobles and knights of the kingdom by this system. Feudalism involved only the nobility. The peasantry had no place in the system.

Manorialism, on the other hand, set up the social and economic structure for the lower classes. Like feudalism, manorialism differed greatly from one country to the next, but the basic concept can be described.

The land of a noble—or lord—which he did not grant to others of the nobility had to be cared for by someone. Since the lands often were vast, the lord had to hire workers to tend the crops and the animals. The entire estate became known as a manor. The lord built his house, the manor house, and chose the best land for himself. This select parcel was called the lord's **demesne**. This land was planted, tended, and harvested by peasants.

The remaining land on the manor was divided into pastureland, wasteland, forests, and farmland for the peasants. The peasants worked their own land after the lord's demesne had been tended. They often paid the lord 50 percent of their own harvest.

The peasants, or serfs, had little future. They were bound to the manor with little hope of moving off the land. The lord of the manor often did little more than provide the land for their huts and crops. The lord, however, could not evict these peasants.

Some peasants, called freemen, could afford to pay rent for land and to hire serfs to work their land. These few peasants also had the right to leave the manor if they could find better land or a better lord.

Feudalism and manorialism succeeded primarily in countries with weak monarchies and strong local government. Countries with strong monarchies eventually moved away from feudalism and toward the development of strong national trade and commerce.

Church. Norman church leaders and practices affected the structure of the English church just as Norman political and social systems had their effects.

Church architecture changed. Church power increased as more and more bishops and abbots were invested with grants of land. The increase of church power led to church intervention in political matters as well as to increased political intervention by government into church matters.

Monastic reforms, the founding of new orders, and the stand taken by men like Thomas à Becket indicated that the church felt the need to return to control over its own affairs, to a divesting of secular power.

The failure of the Crusades and the growth of commerce, cities, and a middle class all led to a spirit of reform seen in men like John Wycliffe. To the common medieval man, however, the church was the center of life. Each manor had a church and a priest's house near the rows of peasants' huts. The church took care of man's spiritual needs from birth to death. This consciousness of God and man is reflected in the literature, the drama, the artifacts, and the architecture of the time. The medieval peasant was not concerned about church politics. He was concerned with finding the strength and the courage to survive a harsh existence. The local church provided the spiritual support needed to give him that strength.

Answer *true* **or** *false.*

2.9   _____   A fief is a noble.

2.10 _____   The demesne is the best land on the manor.

2.11 _____   Serfs were bound to the land and to the manor.

2.12 _____   Freemen could rent land and hire serfs.

2.13 _____   Manorialism was a system of government.

2.14 _____   The church was central to the life of medieval man.

2.15 _____   Feudalism originated after Charlemagne's death.

Changes in medieval society. The Crusades, a series of religious wars, were waged against the Moslem "infidels" in the Holy Land. Kings organized bands of knights to recapture the Holy Land. The First Crusade accomplished the recapture of Jerusalem. The Second Crusade was not successful. The Third Crusade, led by King Richard, accomplished little. No crusades were undertaken to free the Holy Land after 1220.

Although militarily unsuccessful, the Crusades stimulated the growth of trade and banking, the growth of the cities, and the rise of a middle class. Commerce was encouraged by better world-wide conditions: the defeat of the Moslems, the growth of population, and the increase in demand for foreign products. English trade with both the Italian states and with Flanders increased. Italy became a banking center as well as a trade center. Flanders became an important supplier of woolen goods. Certain groups formed trade associations called guilds. Trade fairs were established for national and international trade purposes. The use of money replaced the old barter system and led to the development of banking and monetary systems.

By the eleventh and twelfth centuries, towns were becoming more important. By 1300, London had a population of some forty thousand. Although most of England was still rural, the population move was to the cities. Manufacturing and industry grew, causing growth in urban centers. A middle class rose with the growth of the towns. This new class, made up of shopkeepers, merchants, and tradesmen, gained influence through their growing wealth. Sometimes, these groups joined together to charter a new town and thus attained local independence. These people began to find ways of improving their lives and their political positions. By the end of the Middle Ages, the middle class had become the dominant force.

This growth of commerce, the cities, and the middle class eventually brought about the death of the feudal system in England and on the continent.

Complete these statements.

2.16 Militarily, the Crusades were a _____ .

2.17 Three areas of growth stimulated by the Crusades were:

a. _____ , b. _____ , and c. _____ .

2.18 Trade associations were known as _____ .

2.19 The new middle class was composed of

a. _____ ,

b. _____ , and

c. _____ .

2.20 Feudalism declined as a result of _____

_____ .

31

ENGLISH LITERATURE (1066-1300)

This period of nearly two hundred fifty years saw many changes in language and in literary types. Several dialects were spoken in England. Old literary forms were dying out and being replaced by new forms influenced by continental literature.

Language. The development of the English language after the conquest is complex. Anglo-Saxon was influenced first by Norman French, a blending of French and the Germanic language of the Vikings who had settled in Normandy. Medieval French was also very close to medieval Latin. The upper classes of Norman nobles spoke Norman French as did the tradespeople, workmen, and retainers who had accompanied them. Anglo-Saxon, however, remained the language of the conquered, especially of the common people.

As English kings gained further French territories, new French words from different French dialects entered the language. French and Latin were official court and legal languages, but anyone needing to communicate with the common Englishman would need to know the English spoken by the people.

Little literature of the early part of this period survives. What does survive, however, shows little French influence. The *Anglo-Saxon Chronicle* continued for nearly a century after the conquest. Sermons, religious writings, and historical writings also continued to be written in English.

The main French influence occurs in words referring to matters of state, and to matters of the arts and learning, two areas in which the upper class involved themselves. French became the language of the educated and of the upper class.

Several dialects grew out of this strange coexistence of languages. Middle English dialects vary greatly, depending on the distance of the region from the central government. The London dialect, the dialect in which Chaucer wrote, eventually took precedence and became the basis of modern English. Had another dialect such as the Northwest Midland dialect taken precedence, modern English would be quite different from what it is today.

Answer these questions.

2.21   What language did medieval French resemble? _____

2.22   What two language influences did Norman French combine?

a._____ and b. _____ .

2.23   What was the language of the common people? _____

2.24   What languages were used officially?

a._____ and b. _____ .

Twelfth-century literature. Many new literary forms began to appear in the literature at this time. The development of forms appears to have been gradual when extant literary documents are examined. Some of these forms had been used in Anglo-Saxon literature; others came in from France or were developed by English writers.

The literature of this period also struggled for a language. Some authors chose to write in Latin; others, in French; still others, in English. Some wrote the same work in all three languages.

The late twelfth and the thirteenth centuries saw the rebirth of a true English literature. The fourteenth- and fifteenth-century writers firmly established English as a literary language.

Extant literary works of the twelfth century are scarce. The works consist primarily of sermons, sayings, and historical works, such as the *Peterborough Chronicle*. An important historical work, Geoffrey of Monmouth's *History of the Kings of Britain*, was written in Latin. A famous French version of this text was done by Wace. By the late twelfth century an English-verse translation was done by Layamon and was called simply *Brut*. This work traces the origins of Britain back to Troy (a common practice at this time). Brut, the supposed grandson of Aeneas, led his fellow Trojans out of Greek bondage and arrived on the island that is now Britain.

Other literature of the twelfth century includes sermons and a collection of wise sayings that became known as the *Proverbs of Alfred*.

A final literary form found throughout the ages is the **folk ballad**. Ballads are nearly impossible to date because they usually arise from the oral tradition of a common group of people, are spread from group to group by traveling minstrels or troubadours, and are changed slightly by the minstrel's desire to suit the ballad to the group or by his lapse of memory.

The ballad can be historical or nonhistorical. It may deal with romantic, supernatural, tragic, humorous, or adventurous subjects. Many versions of the same ballad exist because these songs were not written down until the seventeenth and eighteenth centuries. Nearly seventy versions of the ballad *The Twa Sisters* have been noted.

Unlike other forms of poetry, the ballad says very little in many words. A ballad concerns itself with a single incident or scene. The characters reveal the topic of the ballad through dialogue, as in a play. The use of repetition of exact words, or a refrain, is characteristic of this form. This repetition is usually to emphasize the sound of the words and to serve as a convenient memory devise.

The ballad stanza often consists of four lines of iambic pentameter. The first and third lines have four accented syllables; the second and the fourth lines have three accented syllables. The second and the fourth lines rhyme.

Example: Ballad stanza

4 accents: The wínd so cóld blew sóuth and nórth

3 accents: And bléw intó the flóor;

4 accents: Quoth óur goodmán to our goodwífe,

3 accents: "Get úp and bár the dóor."

Many of the early ballads are Scottish and English. The important thing to remember about ballads is that they were written to be sung. They do not read well as poetry; but, read aloud, they give an indication of the rhythm intended for the music.

"Bonny Barbara Allan" is a tragic love ballad that has been sung in many versions. Over one hundred different variations of this ballad have been discovered. It has been particularly popular in several different countries. The original version of the ballad was Scottish.

Barbara Allen's Cruelty

All in the merry month of May,
    When green buds they were swelling,
Young Jemmy Grove on his death-bed lay
    For love of Barbara Allen.

He sent his man unto her then,
    To the town where she was dwelling:
"O haste and come to my master dear,
    If your name be Barbara Allen."

Slowly, slowly she rose up,
    And she came where he was lying;
And when she drew the curtain by,
    Says, "Young man, I think you're dying.

"O it's I am sick, and very, very sick,
    And it's all for Barbara Allen."
"O the better for me you'll never be,
    Tho' your heart's blood were a-spilling!

"O do you not mind, young man," she says,
    "When the red wine you were filling,
That you made the healths go round and round,
    And slighted Barbara Allen?"

He turned his face unto the wall,
    And death with him was dealing:
"Adieu, adieu, my dear friends all;
    Be kind to Barbara Allen."

As she was walking o'er the fields;
　　　She heard the dead-bell knelling;
And every toll the dead-bell struck,
　　　Cried, "Woe to Barbara Allen!"

"O mother, mother, make my bed,
　　　To lay me down in sorrow.
My love has died for me today,
　　　I'll die for him tomorrow."

Author Unknown

Many other popular ballads have been written. This form entertained people for hundreds of years. The Adventures of Robin Hood and of other local heroes have been recorded in song.

Match these items.

2.25 _____ Geoffrey of Monmouth

2.26 _____ Layamon

2.27 _____ collection of wise sayings

2.28 _____ ballad

2.29 _____ twelfth-century literature

a. *Proverbs of Alfred*

b. *History of the Kings of Britain*

c. sermons, sayings, history

d. *Brut*

e. *Roman de Brut*

f. *The Twa Sisters*

Answer these questions.

2.30 What is a folk ballad? _____

_____

_____

2.31 What are the characteristics of the folk ballad? _____

_____

_____

2.32 What is the ballad stanza? _____

_____

_____

Complete this activity.

2.33 Write a ballad. You may simply write one stanza of four lines, or you may wish to write a complete one. Remember to choose an appropriate topic and to use the ballad stanza.

Ⓥ Adult Check _____

　　　　　　　 Initial　　　 Date

35

Thirteenth-century literature. Thirteenth-century literature illustrates a greater diversity of forms and the experimentation with French forms. Attitudes toward chivalry and courtly love had greatly influenced the French literature of the twelfth century. This influence spread to England and to English literature in the thirteenth century.

Chivalry was an outgrowth of the feudal system. A chivalric code of behavior was established for knights. The code demanded honor, loyalty, bravery, and courtesy. It was an ideal rather than a practical reality. Poets, however, created metrical romances based on the ideal. These stories told of the noble deeds of gallant knights such as King Arthur and his Knights of the Round Table. The chivalrous knight is the subject of many tales, poems, and satires from the thirteenth through the fifteenth centuries.

Courtly love is a term coined in the eighteenth century for a type of love described by a twelfth-century Frenchman, Andreas Capellanus (Andrew the Chaplain), in a Latin work.

The tradition of courtly love was spread by the minstrels, or troubadours. According to the system of courtly love, the man sees the lady whose beauty wounds him through his eyes; love's arrows (shot by Cupid) enter his eyes and go to his heart. Only the lady can heal his wound. He must suffer because of his love. He fears to reveal his love to the lady or to others; he becomes sickly and sleepless; when in her presence, he becomes pale, speechless, and confused; he is jealous but constant; he tries to prove himself worthy through brave deeds; and he leaves his heart with the lady when he goes away.

The lady appears to be perfect in appearance. She is described in most *metrical romances:* blond hair, eyes grey as glass, clear complexion, rosy mouth, white skin. She usually comes from a high social position, and treats the lover in a haughty way. To everyone else she is courteous, kind, and refined; she spreads good will to those around her. Like the ideal of chivalry, courtly love occurs more in literature than it did in history. Several of Chaucer's tales contain comments or satires on courtly love. Some of these tales are the "Knight's Tale," the "Franklin's Tale," the "Merchant's Tale," and the "Squire's Tale."

Much of thirteenth-century literature is religious and didactic. Besides sermons, the surviving religious literature in English includes the *Ancrene Riwle* a rule for Anchoresses written by a priest. Anchoresses lived much as a hermit, alone or in small groups, for the service of God. This rule was translated into several dialects and was used for many years.

The religious literature also included several religious lyrics. Religious lyrics (poems) outnumber the secular lyrics that have survived. The main theme of these religious lyrics is the transitoriness of life in this world, much as it was in the Anglo-Saxon elegies. A recurring question throughout these lyrics asks "Where are… ?" Where are the heroes, the famous men, the lords and ladies of old, and so forth. The response is seldom stated, but the implied reply is that they are gone, dead. The lesson for the reader or hearer is that he too will die, that no amount of riches, fame, or power, can save man from the truth of death. Man, therefore, is urged to live for the life after death, not for the things of this world.

Didactic literature, literature written to teach a lesson, was also popular. Many of the didactic poems took the form of a debate. One of the most famous, "The Owl and the Nightingale," has the poet overhearing a lengthy debate between an owl and a nightingale. Scholars do not agree on the exact point of the debate. Several points are argued: youth versus age, summer versus winter, art versus philosophy, monastic versus secular clergy, moral duty versus pleasure, and so on.

Another such debate is the "Debate of the Body and the Soul," one of many debate poems between the soul and the body. The body is usually near death or already dead. The soul berates the body for not living a better life.

Didactic literature also included such things as the "Bestiary," a set of short poems allegorizing animals. In these poems the animal is first described with all its traits, then the allegory is explained. The lion, for example, is described, then compared to the lord.

LANGUAGE ARTS

1 2 0 5

LIFEPAC TEST

79/99

Name _____

Date _____

Score _____

ENGLISH 1205: LIFEPAC TEST

Match the correct answer with the term or name (each answer, 2 points).

1.	_____ Grendel	a.	the head of a convent
2.	_____ Chanticleer	b.	girl representing purity
3.	_____ Pearl	c.	monster
4.	_____ William	d.	Danish king
5.	_____ Venerable Bede	e.	Anglo-Saxon historian
6.	_____ Prioress	f.	peasant
7.	_____ Hrothgar	g.	martyr
8.	_____ freeman	h.	rooster
9.	_____ Geats	i.	ballad
10.	_____ Wyrd	j.	the Conquerer
11.	_____ Becket	k.	the dragon
12.	_____ Franklin	l.	fate
		m.	people of southern Sweden
		n.	landowner

Complete these statements (each answer, 3 points).

13. Anglo-Saxon poetry uses two main devices a. _____ and

    b. _____ .

14. Ballads use a _____ -line stanza.

15. King Arthur was supposed to have lived about A.D. _____ .

16. William conquered Anglo-Saxon England in A.D. _____ .

17. The early Britons mined a. _____ and made weapons out of b. _____ .

18. A major breakthrough in warfare came in the Middle Ages with the development of the

    _____ .

19. The two humble Christians Chaucer wrote about were a. _____

    and b. _____ .

20. The neutral vowel in Middle English is _____ .

21. English is an outgrowth of the London dialect, called _____ .

Write *true* **or** *false* (each answer, 1 point).

22. _____ Chaucer is the most outstanding writer of all times.

23. _____ Hrothgar was the monster Beowulf killed.

24. _____ Barbara Allen was the character in "The Nun's Priest's Tale."

25. _____ Many consonants silent today were pronounced in Middle English.

26. _____ Beowulf died satisfied with his accomplishments.

27. _____ Manorialism is an agreement between two nobles, concerning land and services.

28. _____ Courtly love, written about by Chaucer, was an elaborate system of conduct between men and women.

29. _____ A gnome was a character in the *Canterbury Tales*.

Complete these items (each answer, 5 points).

30. Explain Chaucer's greatest contribution. _____

_____

_____

_____

_____

31. Explain the changes the Norman Invasion brought to England. _____

_____

_____

_____

_____

Answer these questions (each answer, 1 point).

32. What were the literary types used in the Anglo-Saxon period? (list at least four)

   a. _____   c. _____

   b. _____   d. _____

33. What types of literature were written in the twelfth century? (list at least three)

   a. _____   c. _____

   b. _____

34. What types of literature were written in the thirteenth century? (list at least five)

   a. _____   d. _____

   b. _____   e. _____

   c. _____

35. What types of literature were written in the fourteenth century? (list at least five)

   a. _____   d. _____

   b. _____   e. _____

   c. _____

36. Why did feudalism begin to decline in the late thirteenth and fourteenth centuries? (list at least four reasons)

   a. _____

   b. _____

   c. _____

   d. _____

NOTES

The Breton lay, a secular form that came from Brittany and dealt with romance, was a song form that the English began to experiment with at this time. One of the more famous Breton lays to survive is "Sir Orfeo."

Secular lyrics and tales of knights and noble deeds made up the rest of thirteenth-century literature. A renewed interest in alliterative poetry developed late in the thirteenth century and reached a high point in the fourteenth century.

Complete these activities.

2.34 Name at least three types of literature in the thirteenth century.

a. _____

b. _____

c. _____

2.35 The theme of many religious lyrics was _____.

2.36 Chivalry was an outgrowth of the _____.

2.37 Chivalric code demanded a. _____ , b. _____ ,

c. _____ , and d. _____ .

Match these items.

2.38 _____ Andreas Capellanus   a. Breton lay

2.39 _____ "The Owl and the Nightingale"   b. theme of religious lyrics

2.40 _____ "Sir Orfeo"   c. alliterative poetry

2.41 _____ "Bestiary"   d. debate

2.42 _____ "Ancrene Riwle'   e. animal allegory

2 43 _____ "Where are they… ?"   f. courtly love

                                              g. guide for anchoresses

Complete this activity.

2 44 Choose one of the forms discussed in this section. Find more information about it in an encyclopedia or an anthology of medieval literature. Read some of the literature given for this form. Write a two-page paper on the form and the works read.

 Adult Check   _____
                              Initial   Date

Review the material in this section in preparation for the Self Test. This Self Test will check your mastery of this particular section as well as your knowledge of the previous section.

SELF TEST 2

Complete these statements (each answer, 3 points).

2.01   The king of the Danes was _____ .

2.02   The early Britons created _____ a monument probably used as an astronomical calendar.

2.03   A portion of England ceded to the Danes to avoid more warfare was called _____ .

2.04   The archbishop of Canterbury who was assassinated and became the "holy blissful martyr" was

_____ .

2.05   Towns began to grow for two reasons: a. _____ and

b. _____ .

2.06   Members of a group of churchmen who preached the Gospel and ministered to the poor and ill were

called _____ .

Match these names or terms with their correct answer (each answer, 2 points).

2.07   _____ feudalism   a. "Sir Orfeo"

2.08   _____ manorialism   b. agreement between nobles about land and service

2.09   _____ Breton lay   c. epic

2.010 _____ *Beowulf*   d. agreement between noble and serf about land and service

2.011 _____ debate   e. a Norman

2.012 _____ William   f. "Beauclerc"

2.013 _____ John   g. listed in the *Domesday Book*

2.014 _____ Henry   h. "Body and Soul"

                                            i. an unpopular king

Define these terms (each answer, 4 points).

2.015 epic _____

2.016 kenning _____

2.017 alliteration _____

2.018 ballad _____

2.019 scop _____

Complete these lists (each answer, 1 point).

2.020 List the elegies studied in this LIFEPAC.

a. _____

b. _____

c. _____

2.021 List the two early Norman kings.

a. _____

b. _____

2.022 List two major influences upon the Middle Ages.

a. _____

b. _____

2.023 List three other forms of Anglo-Saxon literature you have studied.

a. _____

b. _____

c. _____

Answer these questions (each answer, 5 points).

2.024 What four changes did the language undergo between 1066 and 1300?

a. _____

b. _____

c. _____

d. _____

2.025 Who wrote the *History of the Kings of Britain*? _____

2.026 Why is this British history (2.025) unusual? _____

_____

2.027 What was the *Brut*? _____

_____

_____

_____

2.028 From what language do most of our pronouns come? _____

Score _____

Adult Check _____

Initial   Date

III. FOURTEENTH-CENTURY ENGLAND

Fourteenth-century England was the culmination of forces exerting influence upon medieval society—a world unlike today's society in dress, manners, standards, and technology. Yet through the eyes of Geoffrey Chaucer, you will discover many similarities between his society and today's.

In this section you will study about Geoffrey Chaucer, his England, his life and career, his language, and his works. Through his *Canterbury Tales* you will become more familiar with medieval England and medieval literature. You will also learn more about other fourteenth-century writers and works.

One reason for reading the works of Chaucer carefully is that many parallels exist between conditions of the fourteenth century and those of the twentieth century. Both centuries might be considered times of upheaval. Both reflect the change from an agrarian society with fixed prices and a fixed population to an urban structure based on commerce and industry. Inflation, organized labor, the development of new weapons of warfare, moral degeneration, and skepticism all were issues of the fourteenth century just as they are today.

Chaucer presented a realistic view of mankind. His pilgrims, like people today, were neither all good nor all bad. Although he portrays some saintly types and some rascals, most of the pilgrims seem very much like people we all know—people who have their faults as well as their virtues; people who have problems; people who are human.

SECTION OBJECTIVES

Review these objectives. When you have completed this section, you should be able to:

9. Recognize the Middle English language.

10. Identify Chaucer's writing and to summarize parts of the *Canterbury Tales*.

11. Identify other literary works of the fourteenth century.

VOCABULARY

Study these words to enhance your learning success in this section.

dream-vision   mendicant
fabliau   mock-heroic

GEOFFREY CHAUCER

Geoffrey Chaucer achieved literary recognition and fame in his lifetime. Chaucer has enjoyed great popularity for a period of six centuries. Little is known about his life. Scholars have developed a composite of his life based on his works and on what is known of fourteenth-century society. He was an energetic, enthusiastic man who was able to carry on a successful governmental career and to produce many outstanding literary works at the same time. Second in literary stature only to Shakespeare, Chaucer appeals to people for many reasons. His writing reveals an amazing perception of human nature.

The name Chaucer comes from the French *chaussier,* meaning *maker of shoes*. Chaucer's immedi-

ate ancestors, however, may have been prosperous vintners. He may have been the Chaucer born in the 1340's to John Chaucer and his wife whose name is thought to be Agnes. Chaucer probably served as a page in the household of wealthy English nobles. His acquaintance with many royal and influential people may have begun at that time.

Chaucer's England. Europe was aristocratic in the medieval period. The king wielded the greatest power. Other wealthy and influential people of the day, including John of Gaunt, were at the top of a vast feudal system. In return for land granted them by the king, the nobles were obligated to supply the king with money, equipment, and men in defense of the king's interest. Many lesser nobles were dependent upon these overlords. These nobles supplied the same types of things to their overlords in return for land and protec-

tion. At the bottom of the feudal system were the knights. The economic system of the manor controlled the serfs who belonged to the land and might be bought or sold. These serfs worked the land for their masters. By Chaucer's time, feudalism had begun its decline and was gradually being replaced by industry and trade.

Some of Chaucer's pilgrims in the *Canterbury Tales* reflect the medieval feudal system. The Knight, representing the nobility, held land and served his king. The Squire was training to become a Knight. A boy of noble birth was first made a page. At the age of fourteen he became a squire, and after completing his training and attaining the age of twenty-one, he took his vow and was knighted. The Knight's yeoman in the Prologue was a servant, but a member of the feudal system by his association with the Knight.

The Franklin was a representative of the new rich middle class. Franklins were landowners who may have taken part in the feudal system by contributing money or men rather than personally defending the overlord. The Miller, a resident of a manor or a town, served an area. The Reeve was the manager of a large estate in the lord's absence. The Plowman was a freeman.

The fourteenth century was a period of transition from feudalism to a more modern world. The agrarian economy was being replaced gradually by industry and commerce. This more complex society encouraged the emergence of textile workers and artisans to meet the growing needs of the people. As the decline of feudalism produced more and more freemen, a middle class arose. This period in history was influenced significantly by the growing power wielded by this middle class.

Warfare became a regular part of the people's lives. Beginning about 1340, the Hundred Years' War was both political and economic in nature. With the development of the longbow and the military decline of the English feudal system, the freeman or yeoman became the equal of the knight. A yeoman class of archers proved its worth at the battle of Crécy in 1346, conquering the army of the French as well as injuring the pride of the English knight.

Another factor causing social change was the Black Death, which occurred between 1347 and 1350. The Black Death, or bubonic plague, was a very contagious and deadly form of plague that wiped out almost half of Europe. The already shaky social structure of the times became even more unstable. Edward III attempted to stabilize things by issuing his "Statute of Workers," which fixed wages and prices and required peasants to accept any available work. Social discontent was not so easy to contain, however. The relationship between noble and serf was altered drastically. Some serfs remained on deserted estates; others became paid workers on estates or in the growing cities. Social unrest became apparent in rebellions by the peasants who had tasted a slightly better life and who aspired to even greater social or economic advancement.

Write the letter for the correct answer on each line.

3.1 The fourteenth century was a time of _____ .

    a. war   c. inflation

    b. urban growth   d. upheaval and change

3.2 The name Chaucer came from the word *chaussier* which means _____ .

    a. writer   c. royal page

    b. shoemaker   d. code of honor

3.3 A Franklin was a medieval _____ .

    a. landowner   c. servant to a knight

    b. clergyman   d. estate manager

3.4 The "Statute of Workers" was a measure to _____ .

    a. grant rights to workers   c. create unions

    b. fix wages and prices   d. create welfare

Chaucer's life and career. Chaucer served in military service during the Hundred Years' War. Although captured by the French near Rheims in 1360, he was ransomed and returned to England. He may have served the king during the next few years. He married Philippa Roet, sister of Katherine of Swynford who later became the wife of John of Gaunt. Both Chaucer and his wife served the royal families. Chaucer is believed to have had a daughter and two sons.

Chaucer was a civil servant, that is, he served in various governmental positions during his lifetime. His position required him to represent the king as a diplomat to France and Italy. Chaucer resided in London in a house paid for by the government. By 1394 he had been appointed Comptroller of the Customs and Subsidies on Wools, Skins, and Hides for the port of London. Since wool was one of England's most profitable trade items Chaucer's position was important. He served in this capacity until his term expired. He moved to Kent where he served as justice of the peace. He also represented Kent as a member of Parliament.

A year or two after his wife's death in 1387, he returned to London, taking office as clerk of the King's Works. He was responsible for construction and repair on buildings such as the Tower of London, Westminster Abbey, the royal residences, and other buildings of royal interest. He also was commissioned to maintain bridges, sewers, and ditches along the Thames River in the London area. He carried out the duties of this office for almost two years until he became a deputy forester for the royal forest in Somerset. He apparently retained the favor of the kings since he frequently received small gifts of cash and annuities as well as personal gifts.

In spite of his government offices and the royal gifts, Chaucer was apparently in and out of debt. Records show a claim or two for debts filed against him as well as several loans or advances. He wrote several poems about debt, but he was probably comfortable most of his life.

Complete these activities.

3.5 With a friend find out more about the fourteenth century. See how many parallels you can find between the fourteenth and twentieth centuries.

3.6 Briefly summarize Chaucer's public career. _____

_____

_____

_____

_____

3.7 Find a book with pictures of fourteenth-century England, its fashions, its architecture, or its art. Design an illuminated letter, a design for the page of a book, or draw a scene typical of the fourteenth century. Create a "Chaucer corner" in your classroom, where you may display these designs and any papers you write or books you find on the subject.

 Adult Check _____
                                   Initial   Date

Chaucer's languages. Chaucer's language was the language of London; that is, late Middle English or the Southeast Midland dialect. This dialect, only one of many regional dialects, is the one from which our modern standard English developed.

Not only had words been added to Old English, but many inflections had been dropped. Middle English, however, still retained inflections not used in modern English. The Middle English pronunciation of long vowels and diphthongs is also different from that of Modern English. The following chart demonstrates the correct pronunciation for the long vowel sounds.

MIDDLE ENGLISH LONG VOWEL SOUNDS

Middle English Sound	Middle English Spelling	Modern Pronunciation	Example Words
ā	a, aa	*a* in *father*	*nama*
ē, open	e, ee	*ea* in *wear*	*heeth*
ē, close	e, ee	*a* in *plate*	*feet*
ī	i, y	*ee* in *meet*	*shires*
ō, open	o, oo	*aw* in *paw*	*holy*
ō, close	o, oo	*o* in *holy*	*roote*
ū	ou, ow, ouh	*oo* in *hoot*	*fowles*
ū	u	*ew* in *few*	*vertu*

The short vowel sounds of Middle English are quite similar to those of Modern English.

A final *e* is not silent in Middle English. Called a neutral vowel sound, it is pronounced like the *a* in *sofa*.

The Middle English diphthongs also differ in pronunciation. Notice the usual pronunciation for these sounds in the following chart.

MIDDLE ENGLISH LONG DIPHTHONG PRONUNCIATION

Middle English Sound	Middle English Spelling	Modern Pronunciation	Example Words
ēi	ai, ay, ei, ey	*ay* in *say*	*wey*
au	au, aw	*ou* in *mouse*	*chaunge*
ēu	eu, ew	*ew* in *mew*	*newe*
oi	oi, oy	*oy* in *joy*	*coy*
ōu	ou, ow	*ow* in *owe*	*growen*
ou	o (u), before gh	*aw* in *awl*	*tho(u)ghte*

Although most consonants of Middle English are pronounced as in their modern counterparts, some unusual pronunciations should be noted. The following chart contains these unusual consonant combinations. Notice that the only silent consonants such as *h* and *gn* appear in French words. These sounds were pronounced in Old English words.

MIDDLE ENGLISH CONSONANTS

Consonant	Sound	Example
gg	*dg* in *dodge*	*juggen*
	gg in *dagger*	*daggere*
gh	*ch* in *church*	*lighten*
gn	*g* and *n*	*ligne*
kn, (cn)	*k* and *n*	*knight*
lf, lk, lm	*l* pronounced	*palmers*
wr	*w* and *r*	*wringer*

Write *true* **or** *false*.

3.8 _____ Southeast Midland is a dialect of Middle English.

3.9 _____ England had three dialects of Middle English.

3.10 _____ Chaucer's language was the language of London.

3.11 _____ Middle English differs from Modern English in pronunciation of long vowels, some dipthongs, and some consonants.

3.12 _____ Final *e* is silent in Middle English.

3.13 _____ *Gh* is pronounced *ch* in Middle English.

3.14 _____ In Middle English *h* and *gn* are not silent in words of French origin.

Chaucer's works. By the time Chaucer was well into his twenties, he had already become a poet. His early works include a beautifully written prayer and several love lyrics. Much of his work reflects the French influence of the metrical romances. *His Book of the Duchesse*, a long poem written in tribute to the first wife of John of Gaunt upon her death, combines the French traditional descriptions of the duchess with Chaucer's own art.

His work was influenced by the *Romance of the Rose* of Guillaume de Lorris and Jean de Meun, which sets forth the idea of courtly love. This idea of courtly love can be seen in many of his works, especially in some of the *Canterbury Tales*.

His works also reflect the Italian influence exerted by his contemporaries. Dante's *Divine Comedy* was one of Chaucer's inspirations for his "Hous of Fame." Several of Chaucer's Tales reflect Italian influence. The "Clerks Tale," for example, was based on a tale in Boccaccio's *Decameron*. Boccaccio's poem "Filostrata" also influenced Chaucer's "Troilus and Criseyde."

By 1386 Chaucer had begun working on his *Canterbury Tales*. Chaucer's language is simple and direct. His characters represent a wide variety of the types of people living in England. The tales also represent an anthology of medieval literary types. The setting for the tales is basically English—a group of pilgrims going to the shrine of St. Thomas à Becket at Canterbury. Chaucer had intended for each pilgrim to tell two tales on the way to Canterbury and two more on their return to London. Each tale was to be joined or linked by conversation between the pilgrims and the host. Chaucer died before achieving his goal. By his death in 1400, he had completed twenty-four of the tales, or almost twenty thousand lines.

Chaucer's art is as much arrangement as it is composition of the actual literature. Chaucer began the "Prologue" to his *Canterbury Tales* with the Knight, a man of high morals who was at the top of the social scale. The "Prologue" ended with characters at the bottom of the moral and social scale. Chaucer's characters can be arranged into five successive groups: chivalric or military, regular clergy, middle class or bourgeoisie, humble Christians, and rascals. The first group representing the chivalric or the military, included the Knight, the Squire, and the Yeoman.

The second group of characters is composed of members of the regular clergy: the Prioress, the Monk, the Friar, the second Nun, and the Nun's Priest. This group is introduced by the Prioress. She was the highest of the group in rank as superior of a convent. She was also a representative of high moral standards. Although the Prioress is portrayed somewhat more worldly than was acceptable at the time, no implication of moral laxity is made. The Monk was beneath the Prioress in office as well as in moral character. He openly rejected certain regulations and is even more worldly than she. At the bottom of the regular clergy group was the Friar, an immoral character who became the object of Chaucer's satire. Through his character, some of the church corruption of the times is revealed.

The third group, made up of the secular middle class or *bourgeoisie,* is represented by commercial, professional, and skilled craft members. Chaucer, the Pilgrim, fell into this group although he did not describe himself in the same manner as the other pilgrims. The Merchant was probably the most prosperous member of the group. Merchants of the fourteenth century were traditionally wealthy. Because of his financial success and the respect afforded him by society, the Merchant was the first member described. The Clerk was a poor student who ranked high on the moral scale, even though he was a member of the secular world. The Sergeant of Law was the highest ranking professional in the group. He was highly educated but represented a much more worldly life. The Sergeant was concerned primarily with the business world, in direct contrast with the Franklin who was a man concerned with the luxuries and pleasures of life. Of the middle class society, the Franklin was a highly respected member. He was a country squire or a member of the wealthy landed gentry.

The five guildsmen, sometimes called burgesses, were commercial or industrial members of society. Their prominence was growing as well as their wealth. Their cook was listed with the middle class because he accompanied the guildsmen. The cook, however, was a lower-class person of disgusting appearance and low morals. The Shipman may have been a skilled sea captain but he was characterized as being of questionable morals. He may even have been a pirate. The Physician was a doctor. Doctors of the medieval period, however, were held in very low esteem. For this reason he was placed among the skilled pilgrims. The Wife of Bath represented the lower end of the middle class. She was a skilled weaver. Her moral standards were questionable and her strong opinions obvious. She was a worldly woman.

The fourth group consisted of two members: the Parson and his brother the Plowman. These two members represented Christian virtue and humility. The Parson was the idealized Christian clergyman; the Plowman was the idealized Christian layman.

Match these items.

3.15 _____ Guillaume de Lorris   a. shrine at Canterbury

3.16 _____ Dante   b. list of characters and setting

3.17 _____ Boccacio   c. Divine Comedy

3.18 _____ Thomas à Becket   d. "Sir Orfeo"

3.19 _____ Chaucer   e. Romance of the Rose

3.20 _____ "Prologue"   f. Book of the Duchesse

                                           g. Decameron

Complete these statements.

3.21 The influences on which some of Chaucer's works were based are:

a. "Hous of Fame" based on _____ .

b. "Clerk's Tale" based on _____ .

c. "Troilus and Criseyde" based on _____ .

3.22 The chivalric and military group includes:

a. _____

b. _____

c. _____

3.23 The members of the regular clergy are represented by:

a. _____

b. _____

c. _____

d. _____

e. _____

The framework was interwoven with the tales, linking one to the other. The first link, of course, is the "Prologue" itself. It presents the framework, introduces the characters, and introduces the first tale to be told by the Knight.

The framework was designed to give the reader information about Chaucer and the Host, to reveal more about the characters, to provide motivation for the tales, to provide a device for needed explanations, to provide additional insight into some of the tales, and to reveal Chaucer's feelings about the characters. All of these purposes were achieved by this device, which at the same time created an artistic whole out of seemingly unrelated pieces.

The next link, the "Miller's Prologue," establishes the idea of "paying back" the Knight's noble tale with one of equal interest. The Host asks the Monk to provide the next story, but the crude Miller loudly begins his coarse tale, the first **fabilau**.

In his tale, which deals with lower class people in a comic situation, he makes fun of a carpenter. The Reeve, who has once been a carpenter, takes the tale seriously and proceeds to "get back" at the Miller. The Reeve's tale insults the Miller. The Cook enjoyed the tale so much that he wants to tell his tale immediately. The Host good naturedly insults the cook saying a good tale might help pay back the bad food. The cook begins a fabliau that remains unfinished.

The next link is the introduction to the "Sergeant of Law's Tale." In this segment the Host mentions the time of day indicated by the sun's position and asks the Sergeant of Law to give them a tale. The lawyer then describes the various plots Chaucer has used in other poems. He says that because Chaucer has told all of the good stories in verse, he must use prose. He proceeds, however, to tell a tale in verse.

This pattern is followed throughout the *Canterbury Tales*. Comments about the characters or interaction between them sustain the reader's attention and provide transition for the next tale.

In this section of the Prologue that follows, notice the number of Middle English words that are recognizable. This section can almost be read without the parallel translation.

Here bygynneth the Book
of the Tales of Caunterbury.

Whan that Aprill with his shoures soote
The droghte of March hath perced to the rooté,
And bathed every veyne in swich licour
Of which vertu engendred is the flour;
5   Whan Zephirus eek with his sweete hreeth
Inspired hath in every holt and heeth
The tendre croppes, and the yonge sonne
Hath in the Ram his halve cours yronne,
And smale foweles maken melodye,
10   That slepen al the nyght with open ye
(So priketh hem nature in hir corages);
Thanne longen folk to goon on pilgrimages,
And palmeres for to seken straunge strondes,
To ferne halwes, kowthe in sondry londes;
15   And specially from every shires ende
Of Engelond to Caunterbury they wende,
The hooly blisful martir for to seke,
That hem hath holpen when that they were seeke.
    Bifil that in that seven on a day,
20   In Southwerk at the Tabard as I lay
Redy to wenden on my pligrymage
To Caunterbury with ful devout corage,

At nyght was come into that hostelrye
Wel nyne and twenty in a compaignye,
25 Of sondry folk, by aventure yfalle
In felaweshipe, and pilgrimes were they alle,
That toward Caunterbury wolden ryde.
The chambres and the stables weren wyde,
And wel we weren esed atte beste.
30 And shortly, when the sonne was to reste,
So hadde I spoken with hem everichon
That I was of hir felaweshipe anon,
And made forward erly for to ryse,
To take oure wey ther as I yow devyse.
        But nathelees, whil I have tyme and
35   space,
Er that I ferther in this tale pace,
Me thynketh it acordaunt to resoun
To telle yow al the condicioun
Of ech of hem, so as it semed me,
And whiche they weren, and of what
40   degree,
And eek in what array that they were inne;
And at a knyght than I first bigynne.

The Prologue

Here begins the Book
of the Tales of Canterbury

WHEN April with his showers sweet with fruit
    The drought of March has pierced unto the root
And bathed each vein with liquor that has power
To generate therein and sire the flower;
5   When Zephyr also has, with his sweet breath,
Quickened again, in every holt and heath,
The tender shoots and buds, and the young sun
Into the Ram one half his course has run,
And many little birds make melody
10 That sleep through all the night with open eye
(So Nature pricks them on to ramp and rage)—
Then do folk long to go on pilgrimage,
And palmers to go seeking out strange strands,
To distant shrines well known in sundry lands.
15 And specially from every shire's end
Of England they to Canterbury wend,
The holy blessed martyr there to seek
Who helped them when they lay so ill and weak.
        Befell that, in that season, on a day
20 In Southwark, at the Tabard, as I lay
Ready to start upon my pilgrimage
To Canterbury, full of devout homage,
There came at nightfall to that hostelry
Some nine and twenty in a company
25 Of sundry persons who had chanced to fall
In fellowship, and pilgrims were they all
That toward Canterbury town would ride.

48

The rooms and stables spacious were and wide,
And well we there were eased, and of the best.
30 And briefly, when the sun had gone to rest,
So had I spoken with them, every one,
That I was of their fellowship anon,
And made agreement that we'd early rise
To take the road, as you I will apprise.

35   But none the less, whilst I have time and space,
Before yet farther in this tale I pace,
It seems to me accordant with reason
To inform you of the state of every one
Of all of these, as it appeared to me,
40 And who they were, and what was their degree.
And even how arrayed there at the inn;
And with a knight thus will I first begin.[12]

A KNYGHT ther was, and that a worthy man,
That fro the tyme that he first bigan
45 To riden out, he loved chivalric,
Trouthe and honour, fredom and curteisie.
Ful worthy was he in his lordes werre,
And therto hadde he riden, no man ferre,
As wel in cristendom as in hethenesse,
50 And evere honoured for his worthynesse.
At Alisaundre he was when it was wonne.
Ful ofte tyme he hadde the bord bigonne
Aboven alle nacions in Pruce;
In Lettow hadde he reysed and in Ruce,
55 No Cristen man so ofte of his degree.
In Gernade at the seege eek hadde he be
Of Algezir, and riden in Belmarye.
At Ayas was he and at Satalye,
Whan they were wonne; and in the Grete See
60 At many a noble armee hadde he be.
At mortal batailles hadde he been fiftene,
And foughten for oure feith at Tramyssene
In Iystes thries, and ay slayn his foo
This ilke worthy knyght hadde been also
65 Somtyme with the lord of Palatye
Agayn another hethen in Turkye.
And everemoore he hadde a sovereyn prys;
And though that he were worthy, he was wys,
And of his port as meeke as is a mayde.
70 He nevere yet no vileynye ne sayde
In al his Iyf unto no maner wight.
He was a verray, parfit gentil knyght.
But, for to tellen yow of his array,
His hors were goode, but he was net gay.
75 Of fustian he wered a gypon
Al bismotered with his habergeon,
For he was late ycome from his viage,
And wente for to coon his pilgrymage.

[12]F. N. Robinson. ed. THE WORKS OF GEOFFREY CHAUCER, 2/ed. Copyright © 1957 by F. N. Robinson. Reprinted by permission of Houghton Mifflin Co.

THE KNIGHT

A knight there was, and he a worthy man,
Who, from the moment that he first began
45 To ride about the world, loved chivalry,
Truth, honour, freedom and all courtesy.
Full worthy was he in his liege-lord's war,
And therein had he ridden (none more far)
As well in Christendom as heathenesse,
50 And honoured everywhere for worthiness.
At Alexandria, he, when it was won;
Full oft the table's roster he'd begun
Above all nations' knights in Prussia.
In Latvia raided he, and Russia,
55 No christened man so oft of his degree.
In far Granada at the siege was he
Of Algeciras, and in Belmarie.
At Ayas was he and at Satalye
When they were won; and on the Middle Sea
60 At many a noble meeting chanced to be.
Of mortal battles he had fought fifteen,
And he'd fought for our faith at Tramissene
Three times in lists, and each time slain his foe.
This self-same worthy knight had been also
65 At one time with the lord of Palatye
Against another heathen in Turkey:
And always won he sovereign fame for prize.
Though so illustrious, he was very wise
And bore himself as meekly as a maid.
70 He never yet had any vileness said,
In all his life, to whatsoever wight.
He was a truly perfect, gentle knight.
But now, to tell you all of his array,
His steeds were good, but yet he was not gay.
75 Of simple fustian wore he a jupon
Sadly discoloured by his habergeon;
For he had lately come from his voyage
And now was going on this pilgrimage.[13]

➤ **Answer these questions.**

3.24 What is the framework of the *Canterbury Tales*? _____
_____
_____

3.25 In what month does pilgrimage take place? _____

3.26 How many pilgrims are mentioned in the "Prologue" besides Chaucer? _____

3.27 At what inn did the pilgrims meet? _____

3.28 How many "mortal" battles had the knight fought? _____

[13]Geoffrey Chaucer, *Canterbury Tales*, rendered in Modern English by J. U. Nicholson (New York. Garden City Publishing Company, 1934), pp. 1-3.

The Knight is the highest, both in social order and in moral character. By his initial position in the Prologue, the Knight is held up by Chaucer as a model after which the other pilgrims may pattern themselves. Through the Knight the chivalric ideal may be seen as a blending of the secular and spiritual aspects of human existence. Although the Age of Chivalry had begun its decline, Chaucer's Knight represents chivalry at its best. As a member of the feudal system, a knight owed his loyalty to his overlords and ultimately to his king. A knight must defend with arms his overlords, his king, his country, his honor, and his God. He must be the protector against evil. Chaucer's Knight apparently has been involved in religious wars, rather than political ones. The Knight must have fought against the Moors in Spain or against the Moslems in North Africa and the near East. He could have defended Christendom from northern barbarians. He has the characteristics of an honorable and worthy man. He combines wisdom and strength in war. His motive for pilgrimage is a worthy one. He goes to thank the saint whom he credits for his success in war and his safe return.

The Squire, the son of the Knight, has somewhat more human characteristics. The Squire aspires more to courtly love than to the kind of chivalry practiced by his father. His battles have involved political issues; he has fought against the French. He is primarily interested in impressing his lady with his military accomplishments to win her love. Although this secular emphasis is not at odds with the concept of chivalry, the Squire's interests are much less spiritual than his father's. He is in a different stage of life, still striving to prove himself. His interests include such courtly accomplishments as the composition of music and poetry. His portrait is not so much an opposite to that of the Knight as a complementary one. Considered jointly, both the Knight and the Squire give a full picture of chivalry. The Squire still has time to develop those spiritual ideals held by his father. He is still training to become a knight. The Knight was once a squire, and the Squire will someday become a knight. These two portraits may be taken to be different sides of the same coin.

The Yeoman, the only servant accompanying the Knight, is a little higher in rank than a groom. He is a military man, a sergeant. He is efficient in caring for weapons and equipment. He dresses in green, and carries a longbow and arrows. The longbow was a newly developed weapon of warfare during the fourteenth century. The Yeoman is depicted as a knowledgeable forester, or woodman. As a representative of the lower class, he is included in the Knights' party to show the extent of the feudal responsibility of the Knight.

The Prioress is the first member of the strictly religious group. She is superior of a convent, possibly the one at Stratford-at-the-Bow. She is described as a refined lady. She speaks French with an unorthodox accent. She uses good table manners. That is, she does not drop crumbs on the table, stick her fingers in the sauce, drip food on her clothes, or make greasy smears on her cup. She keeps little dogs for pets. She dresses quite fashionably for a nun—her wimple is pleated and she wears a brooch with the motto "Love Conquers all." She seems to be pretty. Altogether these qualities comprise a complex woman, possibly somewhat more worldly than she should be, and yet so sympathetic, appealing, and kind a person that Chaucer does not criticize her. Indeed, he seems to admire her. Apparently such secular interests exhibited by the Prioress were not allowed to nuns of the fourteenth century.

The description of the Prioress is typical of that used for heroines in the metrical romances. The formula for describing a heroine includes gray eyes, a nose of pleasing proportion, red lips, and a broad forehead. Usually the heroine is blonde, but, in the case of the Prioress, one cannot tell. The Prioress is obviously the highest ranking and a highly moral member of the church group. She is accompanied by three priests and a Second Nun, who acts as her secretary. Her name is Madame Eglentyne.

The Monk is described in more worldly and satirical terms. Although the whole idea of monasticism is to reject worldly things and to embrace the spiritual, the monk is a completely worldly person, who has rejected the spiritual and emphasized the worldly. The monk openly displays his disobedience of his vows. He refuses to do manual labor, which is required in his order, the Augustinians. He enjoys horseback riding and hunting, an activity forbidden by Canon Law.

The Monk is round and cheerful. He loves rich foods and fine clothing. He is described as being bald, "ful [very] fat," with a face that looked as if it had been oiled. He has protruding eyes and a tan complexion—obviously he does not spend all of his days in the monastery. Although Chaucer described him in a satirical way, the monk's main fault is his worldliness; nothing indicates that he is sinful or immoral. He wears fur lined sleeves and uses a gold pin in the shape of a love-knot to fasten his hood under his chin. He wears fine boots and sits astride a fine horse. He loves to hunt. The secular clergy and regular clergy were condemned for such interests by the reformers—Wycliffe and his followers, the Loliards.

Hubert, a greedy Friar, is using the position he holds for his own benefit. He is arrogant, refusing to work with the poor. Hubert deals only with the rich. He is also flirtatious and immoral. Not only does the Friar violate his vows, but he also cheats the church. The

Friar has been entrusted by the church to act as a confessor. Although the church required a confessed sinner to be truly contrite and to perform a certain penance assigned by the confessor, the Friar accepts money from rich sinners wishing to avoid unpleasantness. This money is spent by the Friar personally, or it benefits him indirectly by paying for the construction of his priory. In either case this practice goes against the teachings of St. Francis, the founder of Hubert's order. The Friar is the last of the religious series, lower than the preceding members in rank and in morality. He represents the corrupt conditions of the **mendicant** orders.

The Merchant, a representative of an increasingly important member of society in Chaucer's time, introduces the third group of Pilgrims—the middle class. He is described as wearing a "Flaundryssh" beaver hat, a reference to the wool trade England engaged in with Flanders. The Merchant is described as dignified. His appearance seems to inspire confidence. He is obviously a successful tradesman, not owing money to anyone. He is involved in borrowing and lending as well as in importing and exporting. Chaucer says that he does not know his name. The Merchant represents a rich and powerful class in fourteenth-century England.

The word *clerk* in Chaucer's time referred to a student or to an ecclesiastic. The pilgrim Clerk is a true scholar who neither specializes in training for the clergy, which would create income, nor seeks a career as a teacher or secretary. He studies simply for the sake of learning. He spends all his money on books, having little left for food or clothing. His income seems to have been provided by friends for whom he prays. The beggar student appears often as a standard character in medieval literature. Perhaps as the last line of his portrait indicates, Chaucer's Clerk will eventually teach.

The Sergeant of Laws holds the position of the highest rank a lawyer could attain. Men of this rank were chosen from barristers having sixteen years' experience. Offices held by sergeants of the law included serving as judges of the king's courts, serving as chief baron of the exchequer, or serving as circuit judges. Chaucer's Sergeant appears to have been granted this appointment to office because of the financial success of his practice. He made money by fees, possibly bribes, and probably through real estate dealings. The ironic lines Chaucer uses to describe him indicate that he was not so busy as he seemed. He was more involved in making favorable impressions than in actually accomplishing things. Some people think Chaucer was satirizing a real person, because he was once served a writ of arrest for owing debts. The man signing the writ was a sergeant of the law.

The term *franklin* originally meant *freedman*. By Chaucer's time, however, it had come to mean a member of the landed gentry. An epicurean, the Franklin enjoyed eating. An abundance of foods was always in his house; it "spewed" meat and drink. Even though he loved luxurious living, he is presented as a hospitable host, always ready to feed a guest. As a member of the newly rich class of people, he is not unaware of the responsibilities that wealth brings. He has served as a justice of the peace and as a member of Parliament. He has also been a sheriff and an auditor. This character seems to be a fair and worthy member of society.

The Haberdasher, the Carpenter, a Weaver, a Dyer, and a Tapycer (tapestry-maker) are members of craft guilds, fraternal organizations that were both social and religious in nature. The five men are dressed in the uniform or livery of their guild. These Guildsmen are apparently successful; they have silver rather than the traditional brass trim on their knives. Although near the bottom of the middle class these men are steadily rising in importance.

The Cook was employed by the Guildsmen. He comes at the bottom of the social ladder. He is an unsavory, disgusting person of low morals. The very fact that so revolting a person is chosen to prepare the food for the group is ironic.

The Shipman is possibly a member of the merchant marine that substituted as a real navy at that time. The Shipman is a daring, tough sea captain. Chaucer indicates that he might even be a pirate for all he knew, but he was a "good felawe."

The Doctor of Physik was a practitioner of medieval medicine, a blending of astrology and science. Medieval doctors did not enjoy the respect that modern doctors have. Frequently they were spoken of in joking and disrespectful ways. Chaucer seems to have been kind to his Physician, since he is reported to have healed the sick. The Physician, however, is depicted as a cold, money-loving person. The physician is well-dressed in silk. The Physician's credentials are given in the form of a list of famous people in the sciences and physical sciences whose works the Physician has studied.

The Wife of Bath, a weaver by trade, is an independent person, both in the economic and personal sense. She has outlived five husbands. She is a gossipy, well-traveled woman, but somewhat deaf. She is quite unconventional in behavior and dress. She wears fine new shoes and red stockings. Her head scarves are elaborate; she wears a wide hat, as well as a riding skirt, and spurs. She is a large, gat-toothed woman with a bold, reddish face. She is quite outspoken about her ideas concerning women and marriage. The Wife of Bath represents earthly love.

A person who represents Christian charity is the worthy Parson. He is poor, but dedicated. He is a gentle, kind shepherd to his flock of parishioners. Although the country is too poor to adequately support a priest, he is content with his poverty. He is a learned, yet unworldly man who visits rich and poor alike in all kinds of weather. He believes that he should be an example to his people; he practices what he preaches. Chaucer's portrait of the Parson is in keeping with Wycliffe's ideals, praising those virtues that the Lollards revered, condemning those abuses attacked by the Lollards.

The Plowman, a brother to the Parson, is an honest man. Despite the upheaval in the feudal system, he remains faithful to feudal and moral laws. He is apparently a small tenant farmer. He is a simple man, serving his neighbors as well as God. He represents an ideal Christian.

The first of the group of five rascals ending the prologue is the Miller, a cheat and a brute. Millers in the fourteenth century were considered dishonest. They were reported to have taken three times their legal portion, pushing the scales with the thumb while weighing grain. Chaucer's Miller is not only the usual sort of thief, he is also portrayed as a coarse buffoon who tells crude tales. He is physically strong and stocky. His build would have been suitable for a wrestler. He is described as having a red beard, like a fox or a pig. His nose has a wart out of which grows a tuft of bristly hairs, much like the red bristles of a sows ears. Medieval writers often used physical description to indicate the character of a person. His features indicate a quarrelsome, shameless rascal. He blew the bagpipes to lead the pilgrims out of town.

The Manciple is a steward for a temple, or a group of lawyers. He is able to make money in all his transactions as purchasing agent for a group of thirty lawyers. His ability to come out ahead financially testifies to his skill at cheating.

The Reeve is a subordinate who helped to manage an estate. This Reeve seems to have been higher in rank and responsibility than many. The Reeve is a close-dealing man, cheating his young landlord regularly. He is such a sly thief, or his young landlord is so inexperienced that Oswalt, as the Reeve is called, is praised ironically for lending the young lord his own money. Oswalt is even rewarded with new clothing for his "generosity." Wearing a blue surcoat he rides a gray stallion always trailing behind the rest of the party. Physically he is thin and "colerik." His legs are long and thin as sticks. He is closely shaven and his hair is closely clipped. His appearance is smooth.

The Summoner is an agent for the ecclesiastical courts. He serves papers upon people accused of wrongdoings against the church. This summons required them to appear before the court. The powers of the summoners in the fourteenth century expanded to include spying and testifying against the accused. Many summoners used their office for exerting pressure on innocent people, blackmailing them for personal profit. They also accepted bribes from the guilty.

The Summoner is a reprehensible person, diseased and morally repulsive. His disgusting physical description represents his spiritual condition as well. He is so loathsome in appearance that Chaucer says children were afraid of him.

The Pardoner had hair as yellow as wax. A companion to the Summoner, the Pardoner completes the group of corrupt churchmen. A pardoner's office was to dispense papal indulgences in exchange for donations and contributions to the church charities. A pardoner was not to sell indulgences or to preach as a rule. Some pardoners were laymen. Literature abounds with tales of the rascal pardoner, the one who breaks all the rules to his own good. Frequently, Pardoners are depicted as complete frauds, not associated with any church organization. Chaucer's Pardoner is avaricious, or greedy, and depraved.

Harry Bailly is an enthusiastic, cheerful Host. He had been greeting and serving the Pilgrims in his inn, the Tabard, in Southwark, and decided that he enjoyed the company of this group of Pilgrims so much he would accompany them on their journey.

Although Chaucer the Pilgrim is not described individually in the prologue, he plays an important part in the *Canterbury Tales*. Through his eyes the reader sees the Pilgrims and gains insight about the character of each.

Complete these activities.

3.29 List the five groups of society represented by Chaucer's pilgrims.

a. _____

b. _____

c. _____

d. _____

e. _____

3.30 Describe the purpose of the links. _____

_____

_____

_____

_____

3.31 Select a few classmates to work with. After you have studied various aspects of medieval life, present a panel discussion to your class. Some topics you might want to pursue are 1) travel, 2) religion, 3) medicine, 4) science, 5) industry or trade, 6) dress and customs.

3.32 Write a paper based on Chaucer's example. Create a situation in which people of various backgrounds are thrown together, as in the "Prologue." Describe several of these modern "pilgrims."

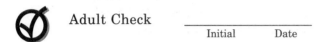 Adult Check   _____
                          Initial   Date

      "The Nun's Priest's Tale" has been enjoyed by millions of people. Based on a fabliau, it is written in **mock-heroic** style. A mock-heroic story is one that pretends to be what it is not. The very contrast between style and content makes it quite humorous. The rooster and hen are described in language as grand as that used to describe Beowulf, King Hrothgar, and Queen Wealhtheow. Chanticleer obviously feels quite important. Chaucer gently makes fun of people so impressed with themselves. Read the following tale, noticing the contrast between the language and the barnyard setting.

THE NUN'S PRIEST'S TALE
OF THE COCK AND HEN, CHANTICLEER
AND PERTELOTE

A widow poor, somewhat advanced in age,
Lived, on a time, within a small cottage
Beside a grove and standing down a dale.

This widow, now, of whom I tell my tale,
Since that same day when she'd been last a wife
Had led, with patience, her strait simple life,
For she'd small goods and little income rent;
By husbanding of such as God had sent
She kept herself and her young daughters twain.
Three large sows had she, and no more, 'tis plain,
Three cows and a lone sheep that she called Moll.
Right sooty was her bedroom and her hall,
Wherein she'd eaten many a slender meal.
Of sharp sauce, why she needed no great deal,
For dainty morsel never passed her throat;
Her diet well accorded with her coat.
Repletion never made this woman sick;
A temperate diet was her whole physic,
And exercise, and her heart's sustenance.
The gout, it hindered her nowise to dance,
Nor apoplexy spun within her head;
And no wine drank she, either white or red;
Her board was mostly garnished, white and black,
With milk and brown bread, whereof she'd no lack,
Broiled bacon and sometimes an egg or two,
For a small dairy business did she do.
    A yard she had, enclosed all roundabout
With pales, and there was a dry ditch without,
And in the yard a cock called Chanticleer.
In all the land, for crowing, he'd no peer.
His voice was merrier than the organ gay
On Mass days, which in church begins to play;
More regular was his crowing in his lodge
Than is a clock or abbey horologe.
By instinct he'd marked each ascension down
Of equinoctial value in that town;
For when fifteen degrees had been ascended,
Then crew he so it might not be amended.
His comb was redder than a fine coral,
And battlemented like a castle wall.
His bill was black and just like jet it shone;
Like azure were his legs and toes, each one;
His spurs were whiter than the lily flower;
And plumage of the burnished gold his dower.
This noble cock had in his governance
Seven hens to give him pride and all pleasance,
Which were his sisters and his paramours
And wondrously like him as to colours,
Whereof the fairest hued upon her throat
Was called the winsome Mistress Pertelote.
Courteous she was, discreet and debonnaire,
Companionable, and she had been so fair
Since that same day when she was seven nights old,
That truly she had taken the heart to hold
Of Chanticleer, locked in her every limb;
He loved her so that all was well with him.
But such a joy it was to hear them sing,
Whenever the bright sun began to spring,

57

In sweet accord, "My love walks through the land."
For at that time, and as I understand,
The beasts and all the birds could speak and sing.
      So it befell that, in a bright dawning,
As Chanticleer midst wives and sisters all
Sat on his perch, the which was in the hall,
And next him sat the winsome Pertelote,
This Chanticleer he groaned within his throat
Like man that in his dreams is troubled sore.
And when fair Pertelote thus heard him roar,
She was aghast and said: "O sweetheart dear,
What ails you that you groan so? Do you hear?
You are a sleepy herald. Fie, for shame!"
      And he replied to her thus: "Ah, madame,
I pray you that you take it not in grief:
By God, I dreamed I'd come to such mischief,
Just now, my heart yet jumps with sore affright.
Now God," cried he, "my vision read aright
And keep my body out of foul prison!
I dreamed, that while I wandered up and down
Within our yard, I saw there a strange beast
Was like a dog, and he'd have made a feast
Upon my body, and have had me dead.
His colour yellow was and somewhat red;
And tipped his tail was, as were both his ears,
With black, unlike the rest, as it appears;
His snout was small and gleaming was each eye.
Remembering how he looked, almost I die;
And all this caused my groaning, I confess."
      "Aha," said she, "fie on you, spiritless!
Alas!" cried she, "for by that God above,
Now have you lost my heart and all my love;
I cannot love a coward, by my faith.
For truly, whatsoever woman saith,
We all desire, if only it may be,
To have a husband hardy, wise, and free,
And trustworthy, no niggard, and no fool,
Nor one that is afraid of every tool,
Nor yet a braggart, by that God above!
How dare you say, for shame, unto your love
That there is anything that you have feared?
Have you not man's heart, and yet have a beard?
Alas! And are you frightened by a vision?
Dreams are, God knows, a matter for derision.
Visions are generated by repletions
And vapours and the body's bad secretions
Of humours overabundant in a wight.
Surely this dream, which you have had tonight,
Comes only of the superfluity
Of your bilious irascibility,
Which causes folk to shiver in their dreams
For arrows and for flames with long red gleams,
For great beasts in the fear that they will bite,
For quarrels and for wolf whelps great and slight;
Just as the humour of melancholy

58

Causes full many a man, in sleep, to cry,
For fear of black bears or of bulls all black,
Or lest black devils put them in a sack.
Of other humours could I tell also,
That bring, to many a sleeping man, great woe;
But I'll pass on as lightly as I can.

"Lo, Cato, and he was a full wise man,
Said he not, we should trouble not for dreams?
Now, sir," said she, "when we fly from the beams,
For God's love go and take some laxative;
On peril of my soul, and as I live,
I counsel you the best, I will not lie,
That both for choler and for melancholy
You purge yourself; and since you shouldn't tarry,
And on this farm there's no apothecary,
I will myself go find some herbs for you
That will be good for health and pecker too;
And in our own yard all these herbs I'll find,
The which have properties of proper kind
To purge you underneath and up above.
Forget this not, now, for God's very love!
You are so very choleric of complexion.
Beware the mounting sun and all dejection,
Nor get yourself with sudden humours hot;
For if you do, I dare well lay a groat
That you shall have the tertian fever's pain,
Or some argue that may well be your bane.
A day or two you shall have digestives
Of worms before you take your laxatives
Of laurel, centuary, and fumitory,
Or else of hellebore purificatory,
Or caper spurge, or else of dogwood berry,
Or herb ivy, all in our yard so merry;
Peck them just as they grow and gulp them in.
Be merry, husband, for your father's kin!
Dread no more dreams. And I can say no more."

"Madam," said he, "gramercy for your lore.
Nevertheless, not running Cato down,
Who had for wisdom such a high renown,
And though he says to hold no dreams in dread,
By God, men have, in many old books, read
Of many a man more an authority
That ever Cato was, pray pardon me,
Who say just the reverse of his sentence,
And have found out by long experience
That dreams, indeed, are good significations,
As much of joys as of all tribulations
That folk endure here in this life present.
There is no need to make an argument;
The very proof of this is shown indeed.

"One of the greatest authors that men read
Says thus: That on a time two comrades went
On pilgrimage, and all in good intent;
And it so chanced they came into a town
Where there was such a crowding, up and down

Of people, and so little harbourage,
That they found not so much as one cottage
Wherein the two of them might sheltered be.
Wherefore they must, as of necessity,
For that one night at least, part company;
And each went to a different hostelry
And took such lodgment as to him did fall.
Now one of them was lodged within a stall,
Far in a yard, with oxen of the plow;
That other man found shelter fair enow,
As was his luck, or was his good fortune,
Whatever 'tis that governs us, each one.
  "So it befell that, long ere it was day,
This last man dreamed in bed, as there he lay,
That his poor fellow did unto him call,
Saying: 'Alas! For in an ox's stall
This night shall I be murdered where I lie.
Now help me, brother dear, before I die.
Come in all haste to me."
Twas thus he said.
This man woke out of sleep, then, all afraid;
But when he'd wakened fully from his sleep,
He turned upon his pillow, yawning deep,
Thinking his dream was but a fantasy.
And then again, while sleeping, thus dreamed he
And then a third time came a voice that said
(Or so he thought): 'Now, comrade, I am dead;
Behold my bloody wounds, so wide and deep!
Early arise tomorrow from your sleep,
And at the west gate of the town,' said he,
A wagon full of dung there shall you see,
Wherein is hid my body craftily;
Do you arrest this wagon right boldly.
They killed me for what money they could gain.
And told in every point how he'd been slain,
With a most pitiful face and pale of hue.
And trust me well, this dream did all come true
For on the morrow, soon as it was day,
Unto his comrade's inn he took the way;
And when he'd come into that ox's stall,
Upon his fellow he began to call.
  The keeper of the place replied anon,
And said he: 'Sir, your friend is up and gone;
As soon as day broke he went out of town.'
This man, then, felt suspicion in him grown,
Remembering the dream that he had had,
And forth he went, no longer tarrying, sad,
Unto the west gate of the town, and found
A dung-cart on its way to dumping-ground,
And it was just the same in every wise
As you have heard the dead man advertise;
And with a hardy heart he then did cry
Vengeance and justice on this felony:
'My comrade has been murdered in the night,
And in this very cart lies, face upright.
I cry to the officers,' said he

60

'That ought to keep the peace in this city.
Alas, alas, here lies my comrade slain!'
    "Why should I longer with this tale detain?
The people rose and turned the cart to ground,
And in the center of the dung they found
The dead man, lately murdered in his sleep.
    "O Blessed God, Who art so true and deep!
Lo, how Thou cost turn murder out alway!
Murder will out, we see it every day.
Murder's so hateful and abominable
To God, Who is so just and reasonable,
That He'll not suffer that it hidden be;
Though it may skulk a year, or two, or three,
Murder will out, and I conclude thereon.
Immediately the rulers of that town,
They took the carter and so sore they racked
Him and the host, until their bones were cracked,
That they confessed their wickedness anon,
And hanged they both were by the neck, and soon.
    "Here may men see that dreams are things to dread.
And certainly, in that same book I read,
Right in the very chapter after this
(I spoof not, as I may have joy and bliss),
Of two men who would voyage oversee,
For some cause, and unto a far country,
If but the winds had not been all contrary,
Causing them both within a town to tarry,
Which town was builded near the haven-side.
But then, one day, along toward eventide,
The wind did change and blow as suited best.
Jolly and glad they went unto their rest.
And were prepared right early for to sail;
But unto one was told a marvelous tale.
For one of them, a-sleeping as he lay,
Did dream a wondrous dream ere it was day.
He thought a strange man stood by his bedside
And did command him, he should there abide,
And said to him: 'If you tomorrow wend,
You shall be drowned; my tale is at an end.'
He woke and told his fellow what he'd met
And prayed him quit the voyage and forget;
For just one day he prayed him there to bide.
His comrade, who was lying there beside,
Began to laugh and scorned him long and fast.
'No dream,' said he, 'may make my heart aghast,
So that I'll quit my business for such things.
I do not care a straw for your dreamings,
For visions are but fantasies and japes.
Men dream, why, every day, of owls and apes,
And many a wild phantasm therewithal;
Men dream of what has never been, nor shall.
But since I see that you will here abide,
And thus forgo this fair wind and this tide,
God knows I'm sorry; nevertheless, good day!"
    "And thus he took his leave and went his way.

But long before the half his course he'd sailed,
I know not why, nor what it was that failed,
But casually the vessel's bottom rent,
And ship and men under the water went,
In sight of other ships were there beside,
The which had sailed with that same wind and tide

"And therefore, pretty Pertelote, my dear,
By such old-time examples may you hear
And learn that no man should be too reckless
Of dreams, for I can tell you, fair mistress,
That many a dream is something well to dread.

"Why in the 'Life' of Saint Keneim I read
(Who was Kenelphus' son, the noble king
Of Mercia), how Kenelm dreamed a thing;
A while ere he was murdered, so they say,
His own death in a vision saw, one day.
His nurse interpreted, as records tell,
That vision, bidding him to guard him well
From treason; but he was but seven years old,
And therefore 'twas but little he'd been told
Of any dream, so holy was his heart.
By God! I'd rather than retain my shirt
That you had read this legend, as have I.
Dame Pertelote, I tell you verily,
Macrobius who wrote of Scipio
The African a vision long ago,
He holds by dreams, saying that they have been
Warnings of things that men have later seen.

"And furthermore, I pray you to look well
In the Old Testament at Daniel,
Whether he held dreams for mere vanity.
Read, too, of Joseph, and you there shall see
Where dreams have sometimes been (I say not all)
Warnings of things that after did befall.
Consider Egypt's king, Dan Pharaoh,
His baker and his butler, these also,
Whether they knew of no effect from dreams.
Whoso will read of sundry realms the themes
May learn of dreams full many a wondrous thing.
Lo, Croesus, who was once of Lydia king,
Dreamed he not that he sat upon a tree,
Which signified that hanged high he should be?
Lo, how Andromache, great Hector's wife,
On that same day when Hector lost his life,
She dreamed upon the very night before
That Hector's life should be lost evermore,
If on that day he battled, without fail.
She warned him, but no warning could avail;
He went to fight, despite all auspices,
And so was shortly slain by Achilles.
But that same tale is all too long to tell,
And, too, it's nearly day, I must not dwell
Upon this; I but say, concluding here,
That from this vision I have cause to fear
Adversity; and I say, furthermore,

That I do set by laxatives no store,
For they are poisonous, I know it well.
Them I defy and love not, truth to tell.
    "But let us speak of mirth and stop all this;
My lady Pertelote, on hope of bliss,
In one respect God's given me much grace;
For when I see the beauty of your face,
You are so rosy-red beneath each eye,
It makes my dreadful terror wholly die

. . . .

    I'll now leave busy Chanticleer to feed,
And with events that followed I'll proceed.
    When that same month wherein the world began,
Which is called March, wherein God first made man,
Was ended, and were passed of days also,
Since March began, full thirty days and two,
It fell that Chanticleer, in all his pride,
His seven wives a-walking by his side,
Cast up his two eyes toward the great bright sun
(Which through the sign of Taurus now had run
Twenty degrees and one, and somewhat more),
And knew by instinct and no other lore
That it was prime, and joyfully he crew,
"The sun, my love," he said, "has climbed anew
Forty degrees and one, and somewhat more.
My lady Pertelote, whom I adore,
Mark now these happy birds, hear how they sing,
And see all these fresh flowers, how they spring;
Full is my heart of revelry and grace."
    But suddenly he fell in grievous case;
For ever the latter end of joy is woe.
God knows that worldly joys do swiftly go;
And if a rhetorician could but write,
He in some chronicle might well indite
And mark it down as sovereign in degree.
Now every wise man, let him hark to me:
This tale is just as true, I undertake,
As is the book of *Launcelot of the Lake*,
Which women always hold in such esteem.
But now I must take up my proper theme.
    A brant-fox, full of sly iniquity,
That in the grove had lived two years, or three,
Now by a fine premeditated plot
That same night, breaking through the hedge, had got
Into the yard where Chanticleer the fair
Was wont, and all his wives too, to repair;
And in a bed of greenery still he lay
Till it was past the quarter of the day,
Waiting his chance on Chanticleer to fall,
As gladly do these killers one and all
Who lie in ambush for to murder men.
O murderer false, there lurking in your den!
O new Iscariot, O new Ganelon!
O false dissimulator, Greek Sinon
That brought down Troy all utterly to sorrow!

O Chanticleer, accursed by that morrow
When you into that yard flew from the beams!
You were well warned, and fully, by your dreams
That this day should hold peril damnably.
But that which God foreknows, it needs must be,
So says the best opinion of the clerks.
Witness some cleric perfect for his works,
That in the schools there's a great altercation
In this regard, and much high disputation
That has involved a hundred thousand men.
But I can't sift it to the bran with pen,
As can the holy Doctor Augustine,
Or Boethius, or Bishop Bradwardine,
Whether the fact of God's great foreknowing
Makes it right needful that I do a thing
(By needful, I mean, of necessity);
Or else, if a free choice he granted me,
To do that same thing, or to do it not,
Though God foreknew before the thing was wrought;
Or if His knowing constrains never at all,
Save by necessity conditional.
I have no part in matters so austere;
My tale is of a cock, as you shall hear,
That took the counsel of his wife, with sorrow,
To walk within the yard upon that morrow
After he'd had the dream whereof I told.
Now women's counsels oft are ill to hold;
A woman's counsel brought us first to woe,
And Adam caused from Paradise to go,
Wherein he was right merry and at ease.
But since I know not whom it may displease
If woman's counsel I hold up to blame,
Pass over, I but said it in my game.
Read authors where such matters do appear,
And what they say of women, you may hear.
These are the cock's words, they are none of mine;
No harm in women can I e'er divine.

　　All in the sand, a-bathing merrily,
Lay Pertelote, with all her sisters by,
There in the sun; and Chanticleer so free
Sang merrier than a mermaid in the sea
(For Physiologus says certainly
That they do sing, both well and merrily).
And so befell that, as he cast his eye
Among the herbs and on a butterfly,
He saw this fox that lay there, crouching low.
Nothing of urge was in him, then, to crow;
But he cried "Cock-cock-cock" and did so start
As man who has a sudden fear at heart.
For naturally a beast desires to flee
From any enemy that he may see,
Though never yet he's clapped on such his eye.
When Chanticleer the fox did then espy,
He would have fled but that the fox anon
Said: "Gentle sir, alas! Why be thus gone?

Are you afraid of me, who am your friend?
Now, surely, I were worse than any fiend
If I should do you harm or villainy.
I came not here upon your deeds to spy;
But, certainly, the cause of my coming
Was only just to listen to you sing.
For truly, you have quite as fine a voice
As angels have that Heaven's choirs rejoice;
Boethius to music could not bring
Such feeling, nor do others who can sing.
My lord your father (God his soul pray bless!)
And too your mother, of her gentleness,
Have been in my abode, to my great ease;
And truly, sir, right fain am I to please.
But since men speak of singing, I will say
(As I still have my eyesight day by day),
Save you, I never heard a man so sing
As did your father in the grey dawning;
Truly 'twas from the heart, his every song.
And that his voice might ever be more strong,
He took such pains that, with his either eye,
He had to blink, so loudly would he cry,
A-standing on his tiptoes therewithal,
Stretching his neck till it grew long and small.
And such discretion, too, by him was shown,
There was no man in any region known
That him in song or wisdom could surpass.
I have well read, in *Dan Burnell the Ass*,
Among his verses, how there was a cock,
Because a priest's son gave to him a knock
Upon the leg, while young and not yet wise,
He caused the boy to lose his benefice.
But, truly, there is no comparison
With the great wisdom and the discretion
Your father had, or with his subtlety.
Now sing, dear sir, for holy charity,
See if you can your father counterfeit."

This Chanticleer his wings began to beat,
As one that could no treason there espy,
So was he ravished by this flattery.
Alas, you lords! Full many a flatterer
Is in your courts, and many a cozener,
That please your honours much more, by my fay,
Than he that truth and justice dares to say.
Go read the Ecclesiast on flattery;
Beware, my lords, of all their treachery!

This Chanticleer stood high upon his toes,
Stretching his neck, and both his eyes did close,
And so did crow right loudly, for the nonce;
And Russel Fox, he started up at once,
And by the gorges grabbed our Chanticleer,
Flung him on back, and toward the wood did steer,
For there was no man who as yet pursued.
O destiny, you cannot be eschewed!
Alas, that Chanticleer flew from the beams!

Alas, his wife recked nothing of his dreams!
And on a Friday fell all this mischance.
O Venus, who art goddess of pleasance,
Since he did serve thee well, this Chanticleer,
And to the utmost of his power here,
More for delight than cocks to multiply,
Why would's" thou suffer him that day to die?
O Gaufred, my dear master sovereign,
Who, when King Richard Lionheart was slain
By arrow, sang his death with sorrow sore,
Why have I not your faculty and lore
To chide Friday, as you did worthily?
(For truly, on a Friday slain was he).
Then would I prove how well I could complain
For Chanticleer's great fear and all his pain.
    Certainly no such cry and lamentation
Were made by ladies at Troy's desolation,
When Pyrrhus with his terrible bared sword
Had taken old King Priam by the beard
And slain him (as the Aeneid tells to us),
As made then all those hens in one chorus
When they had caught a sight of Chanticleer.
But fair Dame Pertelote assailed the ear
Far louder than did Hasdrubal's good wife
When that her husband bold had lost his life,
And Roman legionnaires burned Carthage;
For she so full of torment was, and rage,
She voluntarily to the fire did start
And burned herself there with a steadfast heart.
And you, O woeful hens, just so you cried
As when base Nero burned the city wide
Of Rome, and wept the senators' stern wives
Because their husbands all had lost their lives,
For though not guilty, Nero had them slain.
Now will I turn back to my tale again.
    This simple widow and her daughters two
Heard these hens cry and make so great ado,
And out of doors they started on the run
And saw the fox into the grove just gone,
Bearing upon his back the cock away.
And then they cried, "Alas, and weladay!
Oh, oh, the fox!" and after him they ran,
And after them, with staves, went many a man;
Ran Coll, our dog, ran Talbot and Garland,
And Malkin with a distaff in her hand;
Ran cow and calf and even the very hogs,
So were they scared by barking of the dogs
And shouting men and women all did make,
They all ran so they thought their hearts would break.
They yelled as very fiends do down in Hell;
The ducks they cried as at the butcher fell;
The frightened geese flew up above the trees;
Out of the hive there came the swarm of bees;
So terrible was the noise, ah *ben 'cite!*

Certainly old Jack Straw and his army
Never raised shouting half so loud and shrill
When they were chasing Flemings for to kill,
As on that day was raised upon the fox.
They brought forth trumpets made of brass, of box,
Of horn, of bone, wherein they blew and pooped,
And therewithal they screamed and shrieked and whooped;
It seemed as if the heaven itself should fall!

And now, good men, I pray you hearken all.
Behold how Fortune turns all suddenly
The hope and pride of even her enemy!
This cock, which lay across the fox's back,
In all his fear unto the fox did clack
And say: "Sir, were I you, as I should be,
Then would I say (as God many now help me!),
'Turn back again, presumptuous peasants all!
A very pestilence upon you fall!
Now that I've gained here to this dark wood's side,
In spite of you this cock shall here abide.
I'll eat him by my faith, and that anon!' "

The fox replied: "In faith, it shall be done!"
And as he spoke that word, all suddenly
This cock broke from his mouth, full cleverly,
And high upon a tree he flew anon.
And when the fox saw well that he was gone,
"Alas," quoth he, "O Chanticleer, alas!
I have against you done a base trespass
In that I frightened you, my dear old pard,
When you I seized and brought from out that yard;
But sir, I did it with no foul intent;
Come down, and I will tell you what I meant.
I'll tell the truth to you, God help me so!"

"Nay then," said he, "beshrew us both, you know,
But first, beshrew myself, both blood and bones,
If you beguile me, having done so once,
You shall no more, with any flattery,
Cause me to sing and close up either eye.
For he who shuts his eyes when he should see,
And wilfully, God let him ne'er be free!"

"Nay," said the fox, "but God give him mischance
Who is so indiscreet in governance
He chatters when he ought to hold his peace."

Lo, such it is when watch and ward do cease,
And one grows negligent with flattery.
But you that hold this tale a foolery,
As but about a fox, a cock, a hen,
Yet do not miss the moral, my good men.
For Saint Paul says that all that's written well
Is written down some useful truth to tell.
Then take the wheat and let the chaff lie still.

And now, good God, and if it be They will,
As says Lord Christ, so make us all good men
And bring us into His high bliss. Amen.[14]
HERE ENDS THE NUN'S PRIEST'S TALE

[14]Canterbury Tales, pp. 265-73, 274-81.

Complete this activity.

3.33   Describe an example of contrast in "The Nun's Priest's Tale."

_____

_____

_____

_____

_____

Answer these questions.

3.34   How is Chanticleer caught? _____

_____

_____

3.35   How does he escape? _____

_____

_____

OTHER FOURTEENTH-CENTURY WRITERS AND WORKS.

The fourteenth century was a high point for medieval literature. Many writers besides Chaucer experimented with new forms and wrote poetry that is now considered classic.

One such poet was the author of *Sir Gawain and the Green Knight* and *The Pearl*. Little is known about this author. Scholars can only speculate. They generally agree, however, that the same man wrote these two classic works. Three other poems have also been tentatively ascribed to him.

Both *Gawain* and *The Pearl* have been difficult for the modern reader because the dialect in which they were written was more obscure than the London dialect. Both poems are alliterative; both are very carefully planned.

Gawain is an Arthurian romance in which Gawain, one of Arthur's knights, accepts the challenge of a Green Knight. The large Green Knight bursts into Arthur's hall on New Year's Day and challenges anyone present to strike him a blow with an ax. Gawain accepts the challenge and cuts off the Knight's head. To everyone's surprise, the Knight picks up his head, tells Gawain that he must come to the Green Knight's dwelling the following year to receive a blow, and rides out of the hall, head in hand. Gawain travels to the Knight's castle the following year at Christmas time, receives a warm welcome, enjoys a hunt, and the pleasures of the holiday season. On New Year's Day he faces the Knight and receives a nick on his neck.

This poem is important because of the exact and beautiful descriptions it presents of fourteenth-century English customs and of the seasonal changes in England.

The Pearl is one of the finer elegies in the English language. It combines French and English elements. Alliteration and rhyme are poetic devices used in the elegy. A rather complicated arrangement of stanzas and linking words make *The Pearl* more sophisticated than many modern readers realize.

At the beginning of the poem, the poet is grieving for his lost pearl. He apparently falls into a trance or faint, believing himself to be looking at paradise. As he searches, a beautiful little girl dressed in white trimmed in pearls appears. Her hair is gold; her skin, fair; her eyes, grey. Only then does the reader begin to realize that the girl is the poet's two-year-old daughter who has died.

68

The poet reveals his sorrow at losing her and his happiness at finding her again. He wants to remain with her, but she tells him that he cannot remain. He must die before entering Paradise. Pearl explains that she is one of many blessed now in Heaven. In their discussion she describes Christ's attributes, explains the nature of Heaven, and shows the poet the new Jerusalem from afar.

A procession of celestial beings led by Christ comes into view. The poet is entranced by it all. He wants to die so that he can enter Heaven but he is awakened from his vision. Denied entrance to Heaven, the poet decides to follow Pearl's advice by putting his life into God's hands.

The Pearl is a religious allegory containing both a vision of Paradise and a vision within a vision. The poet combined Biblical principles and orthodox doctrine with some of the elements of the metrical romances. *Pearl's* description and manner reflect the romance tradition. The dream enabled a poet to create a story within a story, lending a believability to the inner story. Dreams were used frequently to reveal religious lessons and other serious philosophy.

The pearl, because of its whiteness and perfection, was the medieval gem for spirituality and Christianity. It symbolized purity, virtue, and truth. The parable of the pearl refers to "pearl of great price." According to the vision, other jewels abound in heaven, but the pearl is the most highly placed. The poet resolves to become a pearl to please Christ.

The *Pearl* is a dream-vision, a poetic device used frequently in the fourteenth century. In a dream-vision the poet, walking in a meadow or wood usually in spring, either falls asleep or is carried away. The poet then has a dream or a vision, which he relates in the poem. The dream or vision itself is usually an allegory.

Chaucer wrote several **dream-visions**. Some are works in themselves, such as the *Book of the Duchesse, The Parlement of Foules* (birds), and *The Hous of Fame*. Others are tales, such as the "Nun's Priest's Tale." Many other authors experimented with this form.

Religious writings were still very prominent in the fourteenth century. Mystics such as Richard Rolle and Julian of Norwick recorded visions and spiritual insights. Robert Mannying compiled a selection of moral tales and called it *Handlyng Synne*. John Wycliffe began his reform.

One of the most popular works of this period was William Langland's *The Vision of William Concerning Piers the Plowman*. This long poem is a religious allegory, a satire, a social history, and a dream-vision. *Piers Plowman*, as it is usually called, was written in alliterative verse. It lays out the essence of the Christian way of life as seen by the author.

John Gower, another moral poet of the fourteenth century, wrote works in three languages. He was called the "moral Gower" by Chaucer. His English work, the *Confessio Amantis*, is the most famous.

Religious drama also reached its peak in the fourteenth century. Drama had begun in the church about the tenth century. The subject of the drama remained religious until the fourteenth century.

Match these items.

3.36	_____	John Gower	a. *dream-vision*
3.37	_____	Chaucer	b. *Gawain and the Green Knight*
3.38	_____	*Pearl*	c. *Piers Plowman*
3.39	_____	Robert Mannying	d. *Confessio Amantis*
3.40	_____	William Langland	e. *Handlyng Synne*
			f. *Hous of Fame*

Complete this activity.

3.41 Select one of the works discussed in this section. Read about the work. Read the work, if possible, in translation. Write a two-page paper discussing the work in relation to Christian principles and in relation to the history and setting of the Middle Ages.

Adult Check   _____
                            Initial   Date

Before you take this last Self Test, you may want to do one or more of these self checks.

1. _____ Read the objectives. Determine if you can do them.

2. _____ Restudy the material related to any objectives that you cannot do.

3. _____ Use the SQ3R study procedure to review the material:
   a. **S**can the sections.
   b. **Q**uestion yourself again (review the questions you wrote initially).
   c. **R**ead to answer your questions.
   d. **R**ecite the answers to yourself.
   e. **R**eview areas you didn't understand.

4. _____ Review all vocabulary, activities, and Self Tests, writing a correct answer for each wrong answer.

SELF TEST 3

Complete these statements (each answer, 3 points).

3.01 Geoffrey Chaucer is best known for his _____ .

3.02 His characters were _____ .

3.03 Three fourteenth-century authors were:

     a. _____

     b. _____

     c. _____

3.04 The use of repetition of initial sounds is called _____ .

3.05 Three pilgrims who were members of the regular clergy were:

     a. _____

     b. _____

     c. _____

3.06 The Normans conquered Anglo-Saxon England in the year _____ .

3.07 The passing on of early culture's beliefs, stories, and history is part of the _____

_____ .

3.08 The "Nun's Priest's Tale" is a a. _____ written in

     b. _____ style.

70

Match the following terms and names with the correct answer (each answer, 2 points).

3.09	_____ elegy	a. a short poem such as "The Anchor"
3.010	_____ ballad	b. a heroic, narrative poem about a national hero
3.011	_____ epic	c. poet
3.012	_____ gnome	d. poem written in an elevated style about a serious subject
3.013	_____ riddle	e. a proverb
3.014	_____ scop	f. a poem written in four line stanzas, about love, death, adventure, and so forth
		g. a poem of six lines

Complete these lists (each part, 1 point).

3.015 List four elements the fourteenth and twentieth centuries have in common.

a. _____

b. _____

c. _____

d. _____

3.016 List four dream-visions.

a. _____

b. _____

c. _____

d. _____

Define these terms (each answer, 4 points).

3.017 dream-vision_____

_____

_____

_____

3.018 fabliau _____

_____

3.019 mock-heroic _____

_____

3.020 comitatus_____

_____

Write the letter for the correct answer in the space provided (each answer, 2 points).

3.021 "Sir Orfeo" is a _____ .

   a. Breton lay   c. epic

   b. allegory   d. play

3.022 "The Owl and the Nightingale" is an example of a _____ .

   a. epic   c. debate

   b. Breton lay   d. history

3.023 Layamon wrote _____ .
    a. "Sir Orfeo"
    b. *Brut*
    c. *Roman de Brut*
    d. *Ancrene RiwIe*

3.024 *The History of the Kings in Britain* was written in _____ .
    a. Anglo-Norman
    b. English
    c. Latin
    d. French

3.025 Feudalism was not a _____ system.
    a. political
    b. religious
    c. social
    d. economic

3.026 *The Pearl* is about _____ .
    a. a treasure hunt
    b. an Arcdurian Knight
    c. a dead child
    d. a necklace

3.027 *Handlying Synne* was written by _____ .
    a. Robert Mannying
    b. Geoffrey of Monmouth
    c. Richard Rolle
    d. Julian of Norwich

3.028 The book that presents allegorical descriptions of animals applied to a moral or religious purpose is _____ .
    a. *Ancrene Riwle*
    b. *Proverbs of Alfred*
    c. *Bestiary*
    d. *Parliment of Foules*

3.029 Chanticleer was a _____ .
    a. widow
    b. hen
    c. fox
    d. rooster

3.030 Beowulf's successor was _____ .
    a. Hrothgar
    b. Wiglaf
    c. Hygelac
    d. Wealhtheow

Answer these questions (each answer, 5 points).

3.031 What language did the Normans speak? _____

3.032 What was the serf's place on the manor? _____

_____

84 / 105

Score _____

Adult Check _____
                  Initial   Date

Before taking the LIFEPAC Test, you may want to do one or more of these self checks.
1. _____ Read the objectives. Check to see if you can do them.
2. _____ Restudy the material related to any objectives that you cannot do.
3. _____ Use the SQ3R study procedure to review the material.
4. _____ Review activities, Self Tests, and LIFEPAC vocabulary words.
5. _____ Restudy areas of weakness indicated by the last Self Test.

GLOSSARY

alliteration. A repetition of initial sounds in two or more words of a line of poetry.

caesura. The pause or break in a line of Anglo-Saxon poetry.

comitatus. In the Germanic system, the relationship between a leader and his warriors, or a king and his lord.

demesne. Manorial land held by the lord, attached to the manor house, and not held by serfs or freemen.

dream-vision. Form of literature in which the poet can tell a story within a story. The poet often falls asleep and has a dream, which becomes his story.

fabliau. A humorous tale popular in French literature.

feudalism. A social, economic, and political system in the Middle Ages in which vassals gave military service in return for land and protection from a lord.

fief. In feudal society, the land held from a lord in return for service.

folk ballad. An anonymous song passed on through the oral tradition; several four-lined stanzas written in iambic pentameter.

Investiture. Ceremony in which the vassal declares his loyalty to his lord and receives his fief.

kenning. A double metaphor, usually hyphenated. Example "swan-road" for sea.

manorialism. A social and economic system in the Middle Ages.

mendicant. Type of religious order that taught and ministered to the poor.

mock-heroic. Literary form that treats trivial matters in an epic style.

vassal. A noble holding a fief from another noble of higher rank.